**"White-hot, ice-cold"** —*N. Y. Times*

*"They knew what it was like to be ripped by the jagged steel of shell fragments, they knew the wrenching Crummp of mortar explosions that could rip your body apart, they knew that the snapping bullets of snipers or machine guns could do more than make neat holes in arms as in the movies (only a flesh wound), they knew these bullets could tear out eyes, smash jaws and cheek bones, or lodged properly in the back, paralyze a man from waist or neck down . . ."*

# Stronger than Fear

Richard Tregaskis

**toExcel**
**San Jose  New York  Lincoln  Shanghai**

**Stronger Than Fear**

Published by toExcel
an imprint of iUniverse.com, Inc.

For information address:
iUniverse.com, Inc.
620 North 48th Street
Suite 201
Lincoln, NE  68504-3467
www.iuniverse.com

ISBN: 0-595-00237-4

Printed in the United States of America

# Table of Contents

To the brave men called

INFANTRY

# FOREWORD

In the late Fall of 1944, I was working as a war correspondent along the Western Front of World War II, trying to keep up with our plunging armored columns as they swept through France, across Belgium and into Germany. The Third Armored Division crossed into Germany at a little town called Rotgen, and shortly after Rotgen our forces hit some sizeable cities in the Rhineland: Aachen, Duren, Eschweiler, Koln.

The street fighting in these German communities reminded me of the jungle campaigning I had seen on Guadalcanal and elsewhere in the South Pacific. The enemy fought hard on his home ground, and everything was close in; the rows of houses were like trees and street-corners were like thickets, and every house was a potential sniper's nest or machine-gun position.

In the city of Aachen, I worked along with a squad of Company B, First Battalion, 26th Infantry, of the Fighting First Division.

It was a great, battle-tested division with one of the best combat records of any of our fighting outfits, starting with the early days of North Africa and on through Sicily and into Europe. I had been with

the First in Sicily through several hard engagements
and I was full of admiration for these men and their
know-how of night-fighting, clever concealment,
skillful use of fires and rapid movement through
rough country.

Now, as at last we were penetrating Germany, the
division was still a marvel of military know-how  But
it was two years after the North African landing, the
battles since had been many and bloody, and casualties came to more than a hundred percent of the
division's original strength in killed and wounded.
The First Division was showing signs of wear.

Being veterans, they knew the chances they
were taking as the companies ploughed through the
streets of Aachen, block by block and house by house.
And those who had been wounded before knew that
the likelihood was they would be wounded, not
killed, if they were hit, because the odds were four
or five to one that you would be wounded, not killed. Those were the statistics that the veterans knew;
they had outgrown the presupposition of the raw re-
cruit that he would either be killed or completely
spared, and that naturally it wouldn't happen to him.

They knew better, they knew what it was like to be
ripped by the jagged steel of shell fragments, they
knew the wrenching *Crummp* of mortar explosions
that could rip your body apart, they knew that the
snapping bullets of snipers or machine-guns could
do more than make neat holes in aims as in the

movies (only a flesh wound). They knew these bullets could tear out eyes, smash jaws and cheek bones, or lodged properly in the back, paralyze a man from waist or neck down.

My company commander was a veteran and he knew these things. His name was Ozell Smoot, and he came from the Deep South. I watched him in admiration, almost with reverence, as he coolly ran his company through the advance into Aachen, through so many blocks per day, through smashing artillery shelling, through black nights in the cellars while tanks roamed the streets with rattling, grinding engines and fired down the boulevards; through the days of pushing through the jungle of the houses, and dodging down the streets to avoid giving the snipers and machine-gunners good shots, and getting aid-men to the unlucky ones who got smeared so their wrecked bodies could be carried to the rear.

What, in other words, are the real values that emerge from a man's character during a war? I had seen enough of war to know that war brings out nobler traits in a man than he might otherwise show in a thousand lifetimes. I knew that men at the front could be more generous, kind, unselfish than I had ever seen them be elsewhere. It was a strange paradox that in a way of life devoted to killing, maiming and destruction of the enemy, men could be kinder and more unselfish and self-sacrificing towards those on his own side than he had ever

ix

been before or probably ever would be again if he survived the war.

Eight months after the street fighting in Aachen I had finished this novel. I think this is the most important book I wrote about World War II because it strikes closer to the heart of war. *The New York Times* book critic Francis Hackett called this book "white-hot, ice-cold": those were the temperatures of my observations and feelings about war as this story worked itself out of the back of my mind.

I believe it stands up well after the years because it hits the basic human values involved in war, aside from politics or patriotism.

The characters show how much I like and admire good fighting men; they are not literal transcriptions of actual people but drawn from many scores of soldiers I watched at work. Captain Paul Kreider is not Captain Ozell Smoot but he stands for many military men who fought the big battle and came out winners, even if they were killed doing their jobs. That's what war or anything else is really about, if you get down to fundamentals. Captain Ozell Smoot was killed about a month after Aachen, in the front line in the Hurtgen Forest, but I saw enough of him to know that he was a winner in the important battle, the one that goes on inside.

HONOLULU, HAWAII
MAY 24, 1961

# CHAPTER 1

IT WAS BLACKNESS, EXHAUSTION. NO DREAMS ON THE spatial horizon; only something of discomfort. Thicknesses, roughnesses of something digging into him, into his back, making him want to move the whole blackness and consciousness on to one side. Welts of clothing rubbing into him at different parts of his body. The same hard cords of something digging into his hipbone. The crusty feeling in the cold clammy feet; wanting to shove it off. In the whirling blackness of existence without time, with time stretching into elastic seconds or minutes—sleep, the sour taste in his mouth; wanting to close his lips over the sour taste; if he could swallow.

Exhaustion hurt the biceps, pinching the muscles against the bone, sharper and harder. A shadow leaned over him, a face; dim light suddenly dawning on the face as he saw it over him. The pressure on the arm was a hand, waking him. Things were rushing into his eyes, objects, the dim light of the room. "Huh? Huh? That was his voice asking the question. He had been sleeping upside down. The bed was turned around. No, it was all right; the same

11

room, the same cold room in a German house, the master bedroom. He was sleeping in the same bed where the master of the house had slept, the smashed house in the German town; sleeping with his clothes and shoes on. This room, this was his company headquarters, the room with the cracked ceiling that dripped rain steadily into the middle of the carpet. The puddle there. The face was leaning over him: Thorson. The voice was saying, "Wake up! Wake up, Captain."

"Okay, okay." Captain Paul Kreider's voice sounded froggy with sleep. "What's up?"

Private First Class Thorson said, "Colonel Tom wants you on the phone."

It was still cold in the dawn light. Captain Paul Kreider shivered. He grabbed his greasy field jacket from the back of a chair, slipped it on, rubbed his chilled body with his arms as he walked over to the field telephone in the center of the room.

He stepped over the puddle of water lying like quicksilver on the soaked carpet. Must have been raining during the night. As he sat down in a chair beside the field telephone he looked up and saw that the crack in the ceiling had lengthened. Along the length of the crack, drops of water poised and fell steadily. If the rain kept up long enough the goddamn ceiling would fall in. There wasn't any roof over it. The goddamn artillery had blown off most of the top of this house, like every house in the city of Unterbach. That was the trouble with this business of street fighting. You knocked the hell out of the houses before you got in, and when you got in you couldn't enjoy living in them.

He was aware that his voice still sounded froggy as he picked up the receiver, but he said efficiently, "Yes, sir."

Lieutenant Colonel J. V. Thompson, the Commanding Officer of the 2nd Battalion, 14th Infantry Regiment, 76th Division, spoke in a tired voice. He always did, but his thinking was quick and effective. "Kreider, just got orders from the boss." That would be General Woodlaw, commanding the Division. "The boss wants us to get to Phase Line D today."

Captain Kreider turned over the acetate-covered map board lying beside the table top and found Phase Line D. It was almost all the way across the town, at the edge of the grid of streets marked to represent houses and city blocks. "I thought we were only going as far as C today," he said.

"Right, but the boss changed his mind. I am sending up Livingood with the dope." Livingood was a liaison officer attached to Battalion Headquarters.

"Yes, sir," said Paul. "Anything else changed?"

"No, same time for the jump-off. Let us know how you're doing."

"Right."

"And listen, Kreider." There was a pause before

13

Colonel Tom went on. "Keep up with Company A and Company C today. I know this is farther than they expected to go, but we don't want to leave any flanks sticking out. Keep B Company up there. Ride on your platoons. Keep 'em going, even if you have to push them yourself."

"Okay." Paul Kreider hung up his phone too. He drew a cigarette from a flattened pack, took a couple of puffs and looked at his watch. It was 5:50. Jump-off this morning at 7:00. That left him an hour and ten minutes. He'd have to get word about the new Phase Line around to the platoon leaders, to tell them they'd have to get all the way through town today instead of just to Phase Line C, which would have been relatively simple. They'd certainly like that! Five or six more blocks to clear before the day was through. So many more houses full of Krauts, maybe streets full of Heinie tanks.

Another day of ducking, sweat and noise. He thought: let's hope the Heinies don't object too much. More kids to get hurt.

Probably the reason for the change was that the German headquarters had turned out to be in the last few blocks, or something. Maybe in the big hotel. That would be nice.

Private Thorson, who had been sitting on the phone during the last couple of hours of the night and had waked Paul, had been listening to the conversation. Thorson listened to everything. He was like

14

a blotter; he always absorbed everything, including all the scandal, and any liquor which happened to be in the vicinity.

"Well, Thorson, you heard all about it," Paul Kreider said. "You know where the platoons are, so go out and tell them we are supposed to get to Phase Line D today before nighttime."

"Yes, sir." Thorson saluted and went out.

One nice thing about Thorson was that he was smart. If he only didn't have such an appetite for schnapps, brew, cognac, whiskey, plain alcohol, or even Aqua Velva, he would have been recommended long before this for OCS. When he was sober he was good officer material. He didn't have to be told twice. He got things straight and he knew everything. But he was a heller when he got drunk, not worth a goddamn.

Well, the hell with Thorson. How about him, the Captain? How about Paul Kreider?

Paul Kreider was not so dumb either. He knew exactly what Colonel Thompson meant when he talked about keeping up with Companies A and C. "We don't want to leave any flanks sticking out," Colonel Tom had said. It was a mild accusation of neglect of duty, reminding Kreider to make sure through personal attention that all the objectives were reached. So Colonel Tom wanted him to ride on his platoons. Ride on them he meant lead them.

Paul Kreider had been wounded twice; once,

15

slightly; the second time, badly enough. Lucky he hadn't been killed; lucky he didn't lose his leg. And he didn't particularly want another cluster for his Purple Heart. He didn't want another Silver Star or a Congressional Medal to be sent back to Suzy Kreider, honoring Captain Paul Kreider posthumously.

He would probably never be the same Paul Kreider who charged ashore at Gela, in Sicily, eager to get into the great adventure, eager to be a hero. Then, when the German tanks had overrun the beach head, he had been the man who took over the 37 mm. gun, after the crew had run away, and fired it and knocked out a tank. When the news correspondent used to nose around, looking for stories, somebody would always tell about Kreider, the One-Man Gun Crew, who was just crazy with courage. Silver Star Kreider—who got a medal. A different, an older, and wiser Kreider, now.

So Paul felt like an old, wise football pro when the coach—that was Colonel Tom—told him, "Push 'em yourself." For Kreider had learned much about the war, and one of the things was that if you sit in company headquarters and push things along from there you are a lot better off personally than if you try to go around on foot amongst your platoons, circulating like a floorwalker in a department store, walking down the spooky streets, looking for this or that platoon while the Krauts pick at you. He had

16

been trying not to stick his neck out, especially now that he had been thinking about Suzy and Dolores, his little daughter, and the people back in the States who couldn't see it as you could over here.

Well, whatever the philosophical considerations, he didn't want another Purple Heart; he was sure of that. He didn't want to push the troops himself, to "ride on the platoons." But it looked as if he'd have to, today. Colonel Tom had seemd so strange about the whole thing. And Paul had a feeling that some of the men in Company B, his own company, had begun to sense his reluctance to stick his neck out, especially Thorson, because he was the smartest, and the closest.

Paul looked up at the ceiling. The crack was widening and the drops were falling faster. Good thing the Krauts hadn't tossed a shell over during the night. It would have caved in the whole damn business. He thought: maybe the fire from the Krauts won't be much today. It had better not be, if my leadership is going to be so inspiring.

He walked to the window and looked out through the curtains over the wreckage in the street. The boarded front of the bank across the street had been blown out. Fragments of the once broad windows were spattered across the pavement, and on the tar surface a tangle of electric-trolley wires lay amongst scattered bricks and flecks of broken glass. He could see the green grass sprouting from the edges of wa-

17

ter-filled bomb holes, old bomb holes from strategic bombing; maybe a year or two old. There was no sound of firing over this silent scene of desolation. "Quiet as a church," he murmured. And he thought that in half an hour all this desolation and destruction would be stirred up again and renewed with violent collisions of explosive atoms when the day's work began.

# CHAPTER 2

WHAM! WHAM! WHAM! THE BIG 76 MM GUNS ON THE tank destroyers at the edge of town were firing into the last five or six blocks of the German city of Unterbach. Probably it was unobserved fire, supposed to soften up the Germans for the beginning of the day's push, firing into some areas where forward observers thought the Krauts might be hiding. Silly idea, that preliminary bombardment. It usually tipped off the Krauts that we were coming.

Or maybe we actually did have a target at this time. Maybe the artillery boys had a nice box seat on a hill some place and were really shooting at something. Although he was nervous and irritable and jittery, as he would be at the beginning of any day's push, Paul could still appreciate the preparations. Maybe it would drive out a few of the Krauts, anyhow.

As long as the shells weren't coming in this way there was nothing to worry about. But the jolting and the banging of the guns nevertheless disturbed him.

Well, there are things to do, Kreider. Got to see

if the first platoon's moving out okay. Company headquarters will be all right. But how about Lieutenant White, the weak man leading the second platoon? He didn't have to worry about the third platoon; he knew Lieutenant Milo would be on the ball.

Sergeant Humphries, assistant to the mess officer, stumbled into the dark headquarters room and fell over a chair and began to curse. "Can't see a damn thing here." He went to the window and pulled aside the heavy wet drapes which had served as blackout curtains when a German family lived in this house. Then he saw Captain Kreider and said, "Oh, I didn't know you were here." The dawn light flooding into the window seemed bright, almost white.

"The sun comes up too goddamn early in the morning," Paul said absently.

Sergeant Humphries demanded, "Want some scrambled eggs," and almost as if in an afterthought, "sir?" There was something about his tone that irritated Paul. Something like the tone Colonel Tom had used when he said this morning, "Ride on the platoons."

But Paul said, "Sure, if you can get that Heinie stove going."

Sergeant Humphries went into the kitchen. It was a wrecked and rumpled, thoroughly looted place which had once been white and spotless and well stocked with preserved vegetables and eggs, like

20

most of the German kitchens. He threw some coal into the oven of the pot-bellied stove; for the gas of the white-enameled stove had long since been turned off. The city utilities had been knocked out by Allied bombings.

Paul watched the water drops dripping from the lengthening crack in the plaster of the ceiling. He was thinking: what is wrong with me? I don't have the zip I used to have. I feel like an old man. This must be war weariness. There are times when I don't seem able to command the respect of the men.

A captain is supposed to be the father of his company, and here you mope and groan around, thinking of yourself; and you are a dope to think so goddamn much about Suzy. Crazy. And you know damn well what Colonel Tom was talking about when he said "Ride the platoons." He was talking about the last Phase Line, when you hadn't got on your objective before nightfall and left C Company sitting out there on the corner with five or six solid blocks of Krauts on their left flank.

If you had been riding the platoons that day as you should have been maybe you'd have got on your objective. You can't keep the kids from hiding in the houses if you don't ride them all the time. You've got to get up and push them individually. Hell, you've got to lead them! You can't do it by absentee direction. You've got to get right down with the men, with your walky-talkies. You've got

21

to circulate like a floorwalker, a floorwalker busy dodging bullets. Looking up at those hundreds of black, staring windows, wondering which one has a sniper inside, wondering whether you will come around a deserted street corner with just your walky-talky men and run smack into a German tank.

That was the trouble with "riding the platoons," as Colonel Tom called it. Of course he, Captain Kreider, had no right to question Colonel Tom, because actually the Colonel would be with the point, the leading platoon, if he were in Kreider's shoes. And even now that he was battalion commander you would see the Colonel doing that more than a few times.

But Colonel Tom didn't have a gal like Suzy or a kid like little Dolores. Or did he? On second thought, he must have a family, too, although he didn't act it. Sticking one's neck out was crazy; that was the trouble with riding the platoons. People got hurt that way. Only yesterday that new lieutenant in C Company, Gunther, his name was—God, he just about got to know the guy's name—three weeks in the company and bang! out; killed; like the four guys in the first squad of the second platoon yesterday, and the bazooka team in the second squad. Whang! That poor bastardly bazooka man losing a leg, blown off. And they didn't think that little kid that got it through the belly would live through it; that's what the aid man said.

Christ, you didn't even get to know the names of your men—they came and went too fast. Pretty different from the beginning, when they were like a family. You knew how many kids they had, and what their wives' names were. Paul couldn't even remember, at the moment, the names of his walky-talky men. Too new. More fresh timber from the replacement depot.

Yeah, it was a rough game. You could get hurt in this game. It was all right for these new kids that just came up and got whanged before they knew which end was up. They only had time to think it was glamorous, just as you thought it was glamorous when you had a week in Sicily, your first week at war. Glamorous certainly wasn't the word for that. It didn't take you long to find out that you could be pretty scared. Then you thought you knew something about it when it caught up with you for the first time, when you were wounded.

Sure, it's not so bad, you thought then, when that burst got you in the shoulder. Iron man—bullets bounced off you. That's what you thought, until Troina. There the promising, vigorous, aggressive platoon leader, named Paul Kreider, found out how he could really get hurt in this game of spit ball.

Maybe he found out too much. Maybe he learned too fast. When he went out on that hospital ship he thought he was going to be reclassified, and he was glad. That's what he thought. So he came in on D-

23

Day, France, crossed Belgium and passed all the off-limit towns without having seen them, and into this hell hole of Germany, this broken stone wall. What a life! No days off in this job; C rations and K. Not even the luxury of a Ten-in-One assortment.

Yet today he'd have to kick his ass out to the point platoons and ride 'em, and keep 'em from hiding in the houses, and keep 'em moving because they didn't like it, either. And so if he got his behind shot off it would serve somebody right. Somebody ... Who? That wasn't very clear, but it certainly wasn't he who would be served right, or Suzy or Dolores.

Oh, well, he talked like a goddamn enlisted man, didn't he? Always grousing, the way the enlisted men grouse about the food or the mail service or this or that platoon leader having done or said this or that, or like an enlisted man that was just homesick. Maybe that was his case, too; just homesick.

Paul Kreider thought about the last letter from Suzy. He was going to shave, but he thought the hell with that. So he took the letter out and read the fourth paragraph. He knew which one he wanted.

"Paul, my darling, I want you and need you so. I want to have you in the bed while you sleep and I can hear your deep, deep breathing, and I can

24

touch you all over without your knowing. But I will know you are everything to me."

He reached in a pocket, pulled out a grimy leather folder, in it was a small studio picture of Suzy: blonde, and with a light skin that seemed translucent. In the other half of the folder, a snapshot of an infant, slightly out of focus. He studied Suzy's translucent skin, the little-girl look of helplessness. He looked at the baby He always wondered if it looked like him It was still too little. He always felt shy about the baby, as if he couldn't believe he really had one—that it was his own.

He put the folder back into his pocket, then went over to the window where a grimy enameled wash basin sat atop a table. He picked up his canteen and glugged a few tablespoonfuls of water into the pan, enough for shaving.

It reminded him of something important. Water. Water for the men. He thought: maybe I am getting to be a complete jerk. Maybe the men don't respect me any more. But I can do this much: I can see whether the truck came up with the water cans during the night.

He yelled out the question to the mess sergeant as he went on with shaving.

"Yes, sir, it came up."

The nature of the question seemed to restore some of the sergeant's respect for Paul. Enlisted men were like anybody else. If they thought you were nice to

25

them and thoughtful of them they respected you more.

This was not, however, the time for philosophizing. There was this job to do. He had been thinking too much lately. Maybe that was what was wrong with his results.

Paul got out a razor and a tube of brushless cream. Even the few drops of water he allowed himself for such purposes felt good on his face. He propped a bit of broken mirror against a vase on the table and was shaving when some one came in the door. He looked to see who it was and started. It was Jerry Bull. Jerry Bull, complete with parachutist jump suit and the grin that he almost always wore. Complete with bull chest and bull neck and flat broken nose; living up to his name, and best of all, still living!

"Jerry!" Paul set down the razor. "You old son of a bitch!"

Jerry Bull never just walked into a room. He barged in as if the passage of his thick chunky body stirred up far-spreading reverberations among the air waves, like a blunt boat forcing her way through the water.

Bull had come up with Lieutenant Livingood, the liaison officer from battalion, who presumably had the dope on the day's operations.

But Paul was much more interested in his old friend whom he had known since days in Newton High School.

26

Paul beckoned Lieutenant Livingood to a chair, and studied Jerry's face. He noticed first that the parachutist was a little thinner about the cheeks, but the grin was still there. He knew that Jerry had been catching hell during the air-borne landing near Barnshaven. Then he noticed that Jerry was wearing silver leaves on his shoulders. A Lieutenant Colonel now, at the age of twenty-nine. "When did you get the promotion?"

"They knocked off all the good men. I was the only guy left," Colonel Bull chuckled. They looked at each other as old friends amongst military men will look at each other, to see what traces recent experiences have left on their faces. Jerry said, "You look a little thin around the gills."

Paul said, "That's the way I feel. You look the same as ever."

Jerry Bull's eyes had that haunted look of a man who has been staring death in the face for a long time. He said, "I am."

Now his eyes were studying Paul's face, the gauntness of the cheeks, the whiteness of the eyelids. "You don't look so hot," he said frankly.

Paul changed the subject. "You haven't seen me since I became a mother. Want to see my kid?" He whipped out the soiled folder carrying the snapshot. "Fourteen months old now."

Fond as he was of Paul, Jerry didn't quite know what to say; he never knew what to say when somebody in the service showed him a picture of a kid. You could only say it was a nice-looking kid; they all looked alike, anyhow. Of course, Paul had written him about the baby, several times. Paul was a buddy who used to share nickels, a buddy whom Jerry, being an older boy, had protected from the neighborhood bullies. Still, the baby looked like any other baby. "Damn cute kid, Paul," he said. That was about all he could say, and mean it.

Paul sensed Jerry's embarrassment, and said, "What are you doing down this way, anyhow?"

The Colonel grinned. "Well, they decided the 408th had been winning the war too fast, so they pulled us out and replaced us with a regular draftee regiment." He laughed. "Like yours. Well, I got tired of sitting on my ass, so I thought I'd drop down and see how you were doing. I stopped in at battalion headquarters and told Thompson I wanted to see what you were up to. Nothing like a change of scenery."

Paul knew that the 408th had been fighting through the Barnshaven gap since they first jumped in, four weeks ago. Paratroopers fighting as regular infantrymen, because, as usual, although there were umpteen million troops in the United States, the same line outfits were still fighting the same war, and there always seemed to be a shortage of good troops. But Paul said, "If you've got a couple of days off, why the hell aren't you in one of those brau-houses drinking beer?"

Bull looked at his friend with level eyes. "I will be," he said. "And I'll find me a woman when I get there. But I knew you were right on the way—and besides, I think I should see the war as it should be fought, for a change. So I left the jeep at battalion and came up with Livingood here. And that's that."

Paul thought: there's no use asking him if he didn't get enough war up at Barnshaven; he's wacky and always has been. He's one of those rare birds that really likes to fight. He even likes this lousy kind of fighting we call war nowadays.

"Well, you'll have a chance to get a good look at the war as she's fought down here," he said, "because we're going to attack in about sixteen min-utes." The remark was superfluous because the 76's of the tank destroyers were banging away so fast and hard that the two men had to talk more loudly than usual.

"I knew that's what all the noise was about," said Colonel Bull. He meant, of course, the preliminary bombardment.

In the soggy living room you could hear the spas-modic banging of the guns going off in groups of four or five, the sounds occasionally overlapping. And then the succession of loud, exaggerated sighs as the projectiles passed over the house. And the cracking of the shells landing and exploding about a quarter of a mile beyond.

"As long as they're going that way," Paul said, "it's okay."

Bull said, "You can't keep on dishing out that stuff without pulling in a couple in return." He meant it as a joke, of course, but he was surprised to see Paul wince at the remark. So he watched his old friend more carefully, especially when he heard a German shell, incoming, wheeze along through the air and land with a crash a couple of blocks from them.

Kreider said, "It sounds pretty close." His arms and legs felt jittery, as if taxed by sudden exertion.

"Not too close," Bull corrected.

Lieutenant Livingood was nervous, too. "Listen," he said, "in case you're interested we've only got a few more minutes. I hate to break up this old school reunion, but Colonel Tom seems to be excited about getting this thing done today."

"Okay, okay." Kreider picked up his map case and studied the grid of the streets as Livingood talked. The set-up was as Paul suspected. Apparently Division wanted to get to the so-called "pistol" building where the German's CP supposedly was located, and finish off the job at Unterbach. It meant they would have to break their necks to get there before sundown. But there was that old story about the 17th Corps—the 76th, 24th and the 18th Armored

30

Divisions—not moving fast enough in cleaning up the last few towns.

Paul knew the political setup in the high command. General Riley, who commanded the 17th Corps, was a weak sister. Apparently Riley had definite orders from Army to finish with the attack, fast. The pressure went down to division, then regiment, then battalion, then to the companies; finally to the platoons. When you came right down to it, it was the platoons and squads that had to do the pushing. It was the old story, let's you and him fight.

"This 'pistol' building should be a pretty tough nut to crack," Livingood was saying, as if Paul didn't know that anyhow. Paul looked at the structure indicated on the map as a black, sharp blob conforming roughly to the shape of a pistol. Once the building was in our hands, the job of cleaning up the last few blocks of the city limits wouldn't be too hard. But first you had to get there.

Jerry Bull followed all this with the natural alacrity of a man skilled in military affairs. Knowing Bull's ability, Paul didn't bother to explain.

Bull said, "Well, what's holding us? Let's hook on and get going."

"How about a couple of scrambled eggs before we go?" Paul suggested. And, without waiting for an answer, he shouted to Sergeant Humphries, "Put on some more eggs, Humphries." Paul knew Bull's appetite.

Now the German shells were coming in more frequently. They weren't close enough yet to warrant ducking. But the last few shook the house. Kreider felt his nervousness increasing. He began to think about moving down to the basement to keep out of the way of the shells. The damn thing seemed to be getting a lot closer with each shot. You could never be too sure. The trouble with shells was that when you heard them, who could tell which way they were going, or whether they were heading in your direction? If you took time to find out, then you might be too late. Certainly if a shell were coming in toward the top of the house he would hear it, but that wouldn't give him time to get out of the door and down into the cellar. Maybe, Paul thought, we should get down into the cellar now. Something was rising inside him. Fear seemed to make his thinking quicker; his judgment grew sharp and fast. His reactions, he was sure, were more highly keyed than those of the others; he knew how suddenly, with how little warning, one could be hit. And then it would be too late.

It seemed very logical to him that he should suggest going into the cellar, just until the attack got underway anyhow. There was no point in being hit up here when he could be safe down there. The company commander ought to take care of himself anyhow, because the company couldn't go ahead by its own momentum. It wasn't as if he were a scout with one of the leading platoons. He was a valuable person in a military sense.

He was going to say something about the cellar when another shell came. And he heard it: Scheeee! Crraash! That one really shook the building. Another one was coming: Scheeee! Crraash! All three officers pulled their heads a little closer to their shoulders. Christ! They're really zeroing in!" Paul said.

And then it came out. He hadn't meant to say it, really. "We'd better get downstairs." He saw Bull glance at him queerly, then grin. "Hell, Paul, we've got to get out there in a few minutes. What the hell's the use of going into the cellar?"

The enemy firing stopped, abruptly. There were no more shells coming from the German side; only the spasmodic banging and sighing of our own projectiles sailing into the German positions. Paul felt a little ashamed. There had been only a few German shells coming, yet he had wanted to run into the basement. He said to himself, "Kreider, you're a jerk." But it had all been so logical and convincing at the time.

Well, there were no more German shells incoming, although his haunted ears strained for the sound. He felt his fear subsiding. And there was still a job to do. He asked Lieutenant Livingood if there were any written orders, and Livingood dragged out some typewritten sheets. Kreider glanced at them, and stuck them in his pocket. He looked at his watch.

"I guess we'd better get going. The hell with the eggs."

He shouted to Humphries, "Eat the eggs yourself," as he tossed three boxes of K rations into his musette bag and slung it over his shoulder. "We can eat these on the run."

He went out, leading the way for Bull. Livingood was going to go back to battalion headquarters. As they passed the kitchen, Sergeant Humphries looked up from his struggle with the stove and cursed. "Sometimes I don't understand that guy at all," he said.

# CHAPTER 3

THEY WORKED ALONG THE EDGE OF A CRATERED STREET, stepping over the irregular piles of smashed bricks and masonry, skirting the bomb craters and shell holes, stumbling occasionally over dismasted electric wires. Paul led the way, moving fast and as decisively as he could, because he was aware that Bull sensed something different about the young infantry captain who had once won the Silver Star. And Paul was thinking; it's lousy for the men if an officer shows fear.

In this case there were only two men following, the walky-talky operators. If he was going to be a good commander and circulate amongst the platoons and ride them as Colonel Tom had ordered, Paul would have to circulate like a floorwalker and he would have to have the walky-talky men with him.

The walky-talkies were his link with the battalion headquarters and the other companies that made up the battalion. One radio was tuned to the company frequency and the other to the battalion CP. Their chatter, the squealing sound of the signals passing across them, the muffled and distorted human voices, seemed somehow comforting to Paul as he started for the first of the platoons. Except for the sound of the two radios, the streets were ghostly in their silence. The preliminary firing of the M-10's and 105's had stopped and there was no sound of any shells coming from the German side. The streets were empty, and empty was the word for the hundreds of windows staring down at them.

The little column was moving in single file; Bull followed the walky-talky operators. He did not walk with Paul because the parachutist knew it didn't do any good to bunch up; that made you a better target.

Kreider would have to check the separate parts of his company—the platoons which composed it —one by one, to make sure they were all pushing, that they were reaching their objective. Probably he would have to go right up to the squads, the smallest units of ten men each, which in turn made up the platoons.

But first he would visit the first platoon, on the right flank of his company sector. He would follow the sound-power phone line leading to the platoon headquarters. He knew that Americans had cleared most of the streets, but there was always danger that a German or two would slip back into one of the houses and get off a burst, especially when there appeared to be only four people in the group of

Americans. So Paul hugged the wall of buildings as closely as possible. The basic theory in street fighting was to keep out of the middle of the street where you would be a better target, to avoid presenting a good shot to the enemy in any of the buildings around, and to restrict to a momentary flash the chance he might have to shoot at you.

The trouble with these maps was that you couldn't be sure you were going in a safe direction. You could more or less follow a line to your objective, but you couldn't be certain that the line had been mopped up completely. However, as long as the sound-power wire was there and could be followed, you couldn't go too far astray, unless it happened to be a German telephone line which you had picked up by mistake.

But Paul wasn't worried—as long as the streets were quiet, the artillery had stopped, and especially since Jerry Bull was with him. They went around a corner and started down another street. Paul studied his map for a moment, holding up the little procession, then moved on. If only he had been riding his platoons as Colonel Tom suggested he would probably know the way better, would be sure of his route. As it was, he thought he was doing all right.

But Jerry Bull stopped him. Bull had a map too which he had picked up from battalion headquarters, and he wanted to know if Paul was sure this was the right way. "It doesn't seem right to me," said Bull. "For one thing, it's too damn quiet."

"No, I think it's okay," said Paul. Bull shrugged and fell into line as Paul started the procession again.

The moment's doubt about the route had upset the walky-talky men a little and they lagged behind Paul as he reached the street corner. He waited for them a second, then started on.

He was getting closer to enemy territory now. In this setup, as in most street fighting, the whole echelon of troops in the field is telescoped and compact. It is only a few blocks from battalion headquarters to your foremost company headquarters and only a few blocks beyond that to your squads. You have to be careful. But this was right, Paul thought. He was sure of it.

He found himself thinking again about that letter. What was it she said about his lying asleep and her being able to touch him without his knowing it? That was a beautiful thing for her to say. There was no other girl in the world like Suzy. The more he saw of other girls, the more he wanted her. Many times he had dreamed about the end of all this filth and misery and danger and of being back and seeing her, of her meeting him at the door, and what she would say. Somehow he had always thought of her as a small defenseless child whom he should protect, although she was actually so very capable of taking care of herself and Dolores.

He had been thinking of her too much. It made the whole business of the war seem so senseless. What would it benefit anyone if he should be killed? And how much misery it would wreak for Suzy! It didn't matter what the war was being fought for; if you were killed the war was lost for you, wasn't it?

He wasn't watching his steps closely enough, and Bull had to stop him short. "Are you sure this is the right line we're following?" Bull asked.

"What? Oh, sure, this is right," Paul said. And then the first shot cracked in the street. The bullet bounced off a wall ahead and zinged over their heads, ricocheting. It was followed by the liquid burping of a "paper-cutter," the German sub-machine gun. The sounds seemed to be coming from ahead, down the street. Paul dived for the wall, ducking behind a fallen, broken cornice of a building, while the others crouched behind him.

Paul's eyes had grown alarmed and apprehensive as he shouted to Bull, "Can you see anything?" He flipped a shell into the chamber of his carbine. He scanned the windows on the far side of the street.

"Don't see them," said Bull. He was calm as he crouched behind the same cornice, and snapped the safety of his carbine.

Paul's mind was racing, and his heart thumped faster: the trouble with this kind of fighting is that you can't be sure where the bastards are; or even, sometimes, whether they are shooting at you.

Once again the burp guns spoke and a string of bullets cracked down the air of the street. They were not close; apparently, again, ricocheting. But if the unseen marksmen were able to get into better position it would be bad for the four Americans.

"We better get back on the main drag," Paul shouted to Colonel Bull, and the Colonel agreed. Paul watched his opportunity, then signaled the walky-talky men to pull out toward the rear. Jerry Bull followed, with a watchful eye bent down the street. Paul hurried around the corner and joined the other three.

"That was a fine job of path-finding," said Bull with a grin. "Better let me try next time." There was nothing of rancor in what the paratrooper said, Paul thought, but it irritated him a little that he had gone down the wrong street. Such a misstep wouldn't indicate anything of itself, for it would be possible for any officer to make a wrong turn. It wouldn't mean that the company commander had not been following his platoons close enough. The only fault was in Paul's letting his mind wander and being homesick when he should have been watching his way.

Returning to the street whence he had started he was otherwise comfortable, and it gave him a feeling of being home. He studied his map as he walked. "I think I'll do better this time," he said. And swinging to the rear, following a safe route which was,

however, slightly longer than the one he had plan-
ned, he came to the first platoon headquarters. The
headquarters was a German house, like all the other
headquarters offices in this business of street fighting. And like all the other houses in Unterbach, it
was almost completely without a top story. The roof
had been partially ripped off by two solid shell hits.

The presence of two GI's in dirty OD's indicated
that it was the headquarters, and differentiated it
from the other smashed buildings leaning on each
other in a pathetic row. There was a small dark
hall way like the hallways of all the German houses,
and like most of them it smelled of tobacco smoke.
There was a faint scent of cooking, probably sauer-
kraut or sauerbraten.

Coming into a house like this always gave Paul's
sensibilities a mild shock. It made him feel that he
was suffering from a kind of amnesia, for it was so
similar to his own German grandfather's house, even
to the flavor of the tobacco and cooking smells. Then
always inside the living room there would be one of
those clocks, and usually a Victorian version of a clas-
sical figure, perhaps Mercury with winged feet and
greaves and an outstretched, very genteel finger on
which one could hang up the key of the clock. There
were always the familiar gewgaws; the whatnot
stand in the corner; the pictures on the mantelpiece,
for the Germans were always strong on pictures
of the family. And the same heavy feeling about

41

the furniture, the substantial pieces, the thick coverings, the dark colors, and the pictures of hunting trophies.

But this was platoon headquarters. Lieutenant Perrine, the platoon leader, was sitting on the sofa eating an apple and studying a sector map of the town of Unterbach. Disposed on the disordered furniture of the room were two or three other members of the platoon.

Lieutenant Perrine extended a bowl of apples to the newcomers, and then when he saw that one of them was wearing a parachutist's jump suit and colonel's leaves on the shoulder tabs, stood up and put down the dish. He nodded politely to the Colonel and went on speaking to Kreider. "The squads are already moving. They should be in position by this time. I'm going to move out in a minute and take a look. Want to come?"

Paul thought about it. He was anxious that Bull should not carry away a bad impression of him. He knew that already this morning Bull had been watching him closely. But, he told himself, unless he particularly wanted to act the part of a hero there was no point in going out with the squad—until things developed a little bit. And Bull, although a devil-may-care paratrooper and a man of great personal courage, would not criticize him for hanging back under the circumstances.

The assertion of his own judgment helped to restore Paul's waning confidence. His mind seemed to be functioning more clearly. More important than going up with a squad would be checking up on White, the weak man leading the second platoon. He ought to run over there and see that everything was organized. Perrine, with the first platoon, was a capable man and there was no point in hanging around, except to see whether the change to Phase Line D had been conveyed by Thorson.

"Did you get the dope on the Phase Line?" he asked Perrine. Perrine nodded. And now that it had been established that the Colonel was only a visitor, the Lieutenant picked up his apple and resumed his eating. "We'll get to D all right today," he said confidently. "These Heinies don't seem to have much fight left in them."

Leaving the first platoon headquarters and heading for the second, Colonel Bull commented on the efficient manner of the young Lieutenant. "We need more guys like that," he said. "He's got guts." Paul glanced at his friend to see if he meant anything personal, but Bull was not looking at him and his face was expressionless.

There was the same tedious, nerve-racking trip from the first to the second platoon. Paul followed streets believed to be secure; but you could never tell. The German sharpshooters might have infiltrated at any place along the line without being stopped. You couldn't physically occupy every house

43

in the city. You had to make a quick check and just trust to luck. So even though they followed back streets, Paul and the others walked carefully and kept close to the houses. But there was no incident. The city of Unterbach was for the time being as quiet as it had been in the Middle Ages.

It was a pleasant contrast to the clamor which Paul knew would fill every street and every block as the infantry platoons and squads, supported by Sherman tanks, worked their way block by block and house by house across the remainder of the city, today.

It was a good thing, Paul was thinking, that the Germans didn't seem to have much fight left in them. A good thing that they didn't know that their forces in the town were about equal to ours, that we were stretched thin, too; almost in a straight line. It was a good thing we had the artillery and the dive bombers to make our bluff stick, and that we had the tanks to make the Germans think we were a lot stronger than we actually were. Also, it was a good thing that the Krauts were mostly "400" regiments, the Sad Sack draftees that had been pulled out of hospitals and replacement camps and factories and thrown in at the last minute to try to hold the crumbling Unterbach-Barnshaven sector. It had been like this all the way across Germany, with the Germans fighting as they could but almost always withdrawing. Fortunately, we had the fire power on our side, as the

44

wreckage of the city of Unterbach, like the wreckage of the other German cities passed through by the American forces, could testify.

But Paul was always thinking too much. He had almost forgotten that he had come to find White and make sure that the Lieutenant would carry out his instructions on time. It was White's platoon that had held up the advance day before yesterday and forced C Company out on the limb with an extended flank.

Lieutenant White was sitting on the front steps of a German house, talking to a couple of his squad leaders. As Paul had suspected, the Lieutenant had been a bit slow in passing out instructions for the push. It was now 7:00. The jump-off was due and the squad leaders were still conferring with White. Paul knew immediately that it was with this sector that he would have to concern himself. The others would probably take care of themselves. "What's holding you up?" he asked.

"Nothing, sir. The dope just arrived a few minutes ago. Thorson was down here."

Paul said sharply, "Thorson was here a half an hour ago. Don't give me that stuff. You'd better get moving. Christ, it's seven o'clock now. The other companies will be moving right about now and if your squads aren't even alerted you'll sure as hell get left behind again. You know we've got to get through the whole damn town today. We've got to get on that objective on time."

Paul knew that he was being critical of the same faults which had been plaguing him of late, but knowledge of his shortcomings didn't help any. Looking at the proposition from a purely selfish point of view, he knew that if the second platoon didn't get on their objective it would foul up the whole plan and leave Company B—that was Paul's company—behind, with C and A sticking out.

This was the time, he knew, to show his courage, if he was going to show it at all. This was the time when the expenditure of courage would be of practical value.

"Would you like to go up and see one of the squads when we get this thing going?" he said to Colonel Bull.

"Sure would." The Colonel showed his even white teeth in a grin. He was a man of great curiosity.

Paul reminded White, "Let's snap it up. Don't forget the squad leaders will still have to pass on the dope to their people before they can push on."

Then he asked White which squad he was going to follow to begin with. Just as a captain of a company did his job well if he rode with the platoons, so the lieutenant of a platoon should circulate among his squads. Paul knew that a squad pushed along by an officer would ordinarily keep moving.

White looked undecided. Then he blurted out, "I

46

think I can handle 'em best from here, from platoon headquarters."

Paul was going to snap at him, but instead he said, "I think you better go on up with the first squad. We'll go up and take a look at the second." He added he would take the squad leader, a sergeant, up with him. He wanted to see what kind of a briefing the squad leader would give the men, anyhow.

As they walked, Paul thought it was somewhat amusing that Colonel Tom had talked to him almost in the same way he had talked to White. He began to wonder whether he was the White of the company commanders. But he was smiling as he led the way toward the second squad. At least he was doing his job as it should be done, and he did not think that he was demonstrating more than the usual amount of fear. But, he thought wryly, he would find out.

# CHAPTER 4

THINGS WERE GOING ALL RIGHT UNTIL THEY REACHED the church. The old ruined church of St. Francis which had been hit by ten or twelve shells was at the edge of the delta-shaped park where it could be seen from the open spaces of the park and the high ground on the north side of the town. The squad leader who led them to the squad headquarters near the church said that it was dangerous to walk in the street without moving very fast. He said that the Germans had been tossing shells over during the night whenever they saw any movement, and they could see practically everything around the church because of the open spaces on the north side.

It was enough to set Paul's nerves on edge, even though the streets were quiet. He found himself thinking of reasons why there would be no point in going up to the second squad after all. The squad leader had his instructions. He would simply pass on the dope to the men of the squad and they would carry out the orders. Why did he, Kreider, have to be up here unless something unusual was going on? If things went wrong then he would have a good reason for rushing up. Otherwise, he would do better to stay at platoon headquarters and not stick his neck out.

Why was it that when things began to get dangerous, his reason always supplied him with such convincing excuses for pulling out? It had happened so many times before. Always, after he had pulled his neck in, he had found that he was sorry and that his so-called logical reasons for withdrawing didn't seem logical at all. But at the time of the temptation the reasoning powers which led him to the rear seemed to be without question very sound.

Now he was watching all the windows, looking down all the alleys, searching out each shadow for some sign of the enemy. Time seemed to be going slower for him; every minute a history in itself, with a beginning, a moment of rising tension and an end. His ears strained for the sound of gunfire, not our own, but the ping of an enemy mortar or the screech of an incoming shell.

Then it came. Schweee! Crrassh! The German shell landed about a block away, with a thud that shook the ground. He saw a dirty gray cloud of debris rising above the housetops; too close.

He had ducked halfway toward the ground when he heard the screech of the approaching projectile. Now he stood up again because he noticed that Colonel Bull had remained upright. In fact, the Colonel was smiling. "Not so good," he said. But Paul was looking for a place of shelter, a culvert or a wall, a tree or a house which might have a fragment of a roof standing over it. His pulse was racing, racing, and he felt furtive, as if he would duck at the slightest whisper.

The hard thing about being under shell fire was that you couldn't tell when the next one was coming. Maybe there wouldn't be any next one, or maybe ten or twelve would fall on you in one huge flood. It was always like this; you were hit when you least expected it. As he had been, twice before. One moment you would be standing here and none would have come in, and perhaps you might have told yourself there wouldn't be any more, and then wham! six or seven on top of you. Or perhaps, on the other hand, there wouldn't be any more for two hours, but the trouble was that you would never know when or where it would begin or end. And any moment, when something did arrive, it could be the end of Paul Kreider, without any warning, without any period of rising tension, without any dramatic structure at all; one moment he would be a reasonably healthy human being and the next moment dead or a hopeless cripple, if he didn't duck, if he didn't watch his places, if he didn't take the proper cover.

And yet in such things there was always the matter of the men with him. Yes, a captain was the father of his company. And in a moment the men would watch to see whether he was going to duck when

51

a shell came, whether he was going to take care of himself before he took care of them; in short, whether or not they should be scared was determined by the example which the captain showed them.

So when he heard another coming—first the faint screech rising swiftly to a howl, like a jeep screeching around a corner—he didn't hit the ground. He didn't even duck. He stayed upright and waited for the shell to come. The time seemed to go slowly as the screaming projectile came closer and the sound louder and louder. So many thoughts were racing through his head. The few seconds of the sound seemed to be hours. He was wondering if he would have time to get down if the shell came close. Just another second or fraction of a second he hesitated, and then the unbearable banshee wail of the shell grew louder and he abandoned his resolution and found himself abruptly on the pavement. Schweee! Crrassh! That one was no closer than the last, but Paul's concern was multiplying. His heart beat so fast that it seemed altogether out of control. Then he found that he was lying on the tar surface of the street, looking down at the flecks of broken glass spattered on the pavement, and he was staying there because more shells were coming.

Suddenly he seemed to forget about everything —about Colonel Bull and the two walky-talky men, the sergeant and the first squad and the second platoon, and even the Division. He was running back toward the wall, the nearest wall of the nearest house, and the shells were screeching in and shaking the earth. He ran ten or twelve yards and fell behind a pile of bricks, then saw a cellar door with steps going down, and slid down the steps, banging his knees, but thinking only of his gladness at being out of the street.

Then he thought of the others, but he noticed that they were running toward him as the shells tumbled into the block beyond—all except Colonel Bull. Bull had succumbed only to the extent of crouching low. From this position he was calmly watching the clouds of debris rising from the three or four shell bursts in the next block. Meanwhile the enlisted men slid down the cellar steps and lay beside Paul as two or three more shells screeched into the opposite side of the street. Still Jerry Bull remained crouching.

Suddenly the firing stopped. It was always that way with artillery shelling. The beginning and ending of it didn't seem to have any causal explanation. Sometimes, when it was the worst, it stopped without warning. Probably that was because the shells weren't directed at *you* at all, or perhaps because the flashes of the enemy battery had been spotted by our own artillery observers. But you could never tell.

When a few seconds had elaspsed and Bull was standing again, Paul hurried back to him. Bull noticed that his friend's eyes had the haunted look of a man in the midst of great alarm or fear. So he said, by way of exerting a calming influence, "Jesus Christ! They weren't that close! They were way over on the other side of the block."

Paul knew it was a criticism, but said simply, "Well, I don't think it will do us any good to hang around this street, anyhow. All we're doing here is wasting time. I think we'd better move out." He was struggling for an argument, a reason, why he should move, and then he had it. In the silence after the burst of German firing, they could hear the water-fall-like clatter of small-arms fire on both the left and right flanks, and the heavier booming of the tanks, M-10's and bazookas going into action. It was practically all our firing, the deeper-toned American small arms and our artillery. He knew that the jumping-off had begun, that the attack was beginning as scheduled for the day.

"I guess things are beginning to happen," he said to Bull, while he still kept an apprehensive eye on the sky. "I think we better get on back to the platoon headquarters and see what gives. I think the sergeant will be able to take care of this sector all right."

"But, sir, the squad is just around the corner. We could get over there in a minute," said the sergeant, who had climbed out of the cellar and regained his composure.

54

"Oh, is it?" Paul's voice seemed very uncertain and undecided. It now began to appear to him when the menace of shells was no longer present that he had played the coward in suggesting that they should pull back to platoon headquarters. "Well, I guess if it's as close as that we'd better go on up," he said gruffly.

But the striking, hard bruising impact of fear rose again as he thought of the fact that probably the squad headquarters was around the corner where the shells had just landed. Perhaps the next bracket of shells would land squarely there. Yet he thought he could see Jerry Bull looking at him with something almost contemptuous in his glance. So he said, "Well, let's go, then."

The squad headquarters had not been directly hit by the shells. They had landed across the street, smashing in the front of a gray-stone German house and tearing apart the flagstone sidewalks, littering the street surface with bricks and broken bits of rubble; and hitting some of the members of the squad with jagged splinters of high explosives.

Paul heard them crying as he came around the corner. Three of the men of the squad had been out in the street, and they had all been hit. One lay still in the street, green-faced, cold, staring up at the sky, arms outstretched. The other two were moving and moaning. It was always horrible to hear the sounds made by a wounded man. But automatically he snatched his first-aid package from his webbing belt and began to mop blood from the torn shoulder of one of the men where a shell fragment had ripped off the laminated layers of muscle and skin, showing the gray bone underneath. The shock of the sight was doubly strong, for he felt that if he had arrived at the squad headquarters a few seconds before he too would have been lying on the pavement in his own blood, perhaps with an arm or a foot or a leg torn from his body. He had seen enough of these things, especially in the hospitals.

Colonel Bull began to shout for the members of the squad who must be in one of the houses in the vicinity. Now that the shelling seemed to have lulled they came out and helped. Paul told a runner to go back and get a litter squad at platoon headquarters, then decided abruptly that it would bet better, much better, for him to go back himself. The sergeant could handle the squad from here on. Since there were wounded here and there was other business to attend to in the other platoons, he should check back to company headquarters and see what the latest developments might be, to see whether the platoons of the company were making satisfactory progress. He explained this to Jerry Bull and got a grudging assent. Paul noticed that Bull was watching when he cautioned the sergeant to get onto the objective, whatever might develop.

# CHAPTER 5

When he got to platoon headquarters and dispatched a litter squad there was no real reason to go farther to the rear, but Paul said to Jerry, "I think I better check in with company headquarters to see what's cooking."

Jerry Bull said abruptly, "I don't know what's got into you, Paul. You're acting like a nut. There's no reason to get back there when you've got your walky-talkies right with you. Why don't you pick up headquarters and the other companies and get the latest dope direct?"

Paul had almost forgotten that he still had his two walky-talky men with him. If he had been working as he should have worked during the last few days, of course he would have been in the habit of using the walky-takies for constant communication. As it was, he was embarrassed—and afraid.

All around him the sounds of battle seemed to be growing louder and louder. Besides the heavy clamor of American arms, the swift liquid cadence of German burp guns could be heard. The air seemed full of danger pressing in from many directions. His nerves were drawing tighter.

Jerry Bull looked into Paul's eyes and saw something there which was not pleasant. Jerry had seen that look before: the quick-shifting eyes, the nervous movements of the neck—the look of a cornered animal. Jerry had seen other men break under the hammering of the front, and he did not want his friend to be broken this way. He had seen strong men fall into helpless, blubbering masses of jelly, their strength and will suddenly gone, when the pounding on their taut nerves went on too long, too intensely. Everyone had a breaking point, and the breaking point came sooner if you had a family, someone in the States, someone you wanted very much to go home to.

Jerry Bull was a man of decision and action. He knew that something would have to be done for his friend, and he intended to do it. So he stopped the walky-talky men, told them to write down all calls from battalion, and anything startling from A or C Company. Then he said to Paul, "You and I are going to have a talk." He sounded like a big brother —as he had so many times before when they were kids. But that was unimportant. He led the way into the front hall of a German house, to get Paul away from the hearing range of the men. There was a settee in the living room of the house and Paul

58

sank onto it, while Bull brushed aside the plaster fragments from the top of a table, and sat down.

"What's all the mystery, Jerry?"

Jerry was at a loss when it came to putting so complex a matter into words. But he said, "Paul, I think you're thinking of something besides yourself. Sometimes I think that way myself; not that much, but like that." He stumbled on, "Lots of the boys think of their girls, and their kids, too."

He paused. This was a tough job. Sweat was breaking out on his forehead under the leather band of his helmet. He said, "There are some things you have to figure out for yourself. There's something wrong with you today—must have been for a while." He thought a moment. "I don't want you to make a fool of yourself. It's hard for me to say it. But I want you to sit and think about it for 'a couple of minutes, take time off—and I'll stay outside with the walky-talky men, in case anything develops."

Paul knew what he was talking about, definitely enough. His thoughts shifted to Suzy and Dolores. He sat there disconsolately, looking around at the furnishings, the typical German fixtures of this German home in the city of Unterbach. Perhaps he really was thinking too much of his own home, of Suzy. He wasn't thinking enough of his men: how to fight his men, how to act like an officer.

Outside, the battle noises were mounting in volume. There was an almost steady cascade of small-arms fire and somewhere within a block or two there were the large sharp explosions of tank cannon or bazooka shells—you couldn't be sure which. Paul studied the pictures, the inevitable pictures on the mantelpiece, the grown-up members of the family portrayed by an old-fashioned photographer, and the snapshots of the little children. The pictures of the babies made him think of little Dolores. whom he had never seen. Then he thought of what Jerry Bull had said, "Don't think of other people; think of yourself." Bull had a way of putting his finger on the heart of things, even though he was largely inarticulate. After all, perhaps Paul was thinking too much about two other people, however close they might be, and thinking too little of the fact that he was acting like an ass. No man should show fear, especially no officer, as he had today.

This was how he should think of himself; no matter what the chances of not coming through, whatever the cost might be, he simply must keep his self-respect. He had thought of it before and forgotten it. He wanted it to be clear in his own mind as it used to be, because he had forgotten it in the stress and hurry of the war. At first when he had gone into action he had acted creditably, probably because he had the unutterable confidence, which comes to men in their first actions, that he would never be hit; that other people would be the casualties. That almost sublime self-confidence had disappeared. It had ebbed away gradually as he saw more of his friends hurt. Then when he himself had been so badly wounded it had completely deserted him. Now, perhaps, he could replace it with a new understanding. He might never regain the same confidence that he would not be hurt again, but he could be sure of one thing. That was that bravery would survive, that moments of bravery and self-sacrifice, honor and decency were probably the only lasting things in this life of danger and death. He had thought about the impermanence of things so many times, about the fact that one moment his friends would be living human beings with personalities, and the next moment nothing but mutilated flesh, like meat in a butcher shop, with every trace of the personality gone, flown away. But he had thought often that the body which remained was nothing, and that the qualities of the spirit were permanent.

Probably it was the life of the infantrymen in a rifle company which had given him the sense of the impermanence of physical things. He knew, as every infantryman realized sooner or later, that if you stayed in an infantry rifle company too long you had two choices, or rather, two things could happen to you: in either case, you would eventually get hurt. If you were only slightly hurt the chances were you would be sent back to your infantry outfit until you were either so seriously hurt that you would be no use to anyone; or, of course, you might get killed.

61

He had not thought of all this in such a concrete way before, but it was true. Everyone had to make the adjustment to these possibilties, even though he might not be able to define them so clearly. Jerry Bull, the swashbuckling, adventurous man of action, must have come to some similar resolution, some rational attitude toward the chances he was taking. Paul knew that in the case of Bull there was a basically reckless attitude toward life. He knew Jerry's history, a history of frustration and defeat, both in love and the jobs at which he had worked. One of the reasons that he had moved so fast in the Army was his love of action and his reckless attitude toward his own life or death.

Definitely, Jerry Bull had the sense of personal dignity which Paul Kreider had lacked so severely during the last few weeks. It was Paul's concern for his own life, his fear of losing that life that had led him to be a poor soldier. Probably at the bottom, the structure of his cowardice was built on his wife and the daughter whom he had never seen. He had wanted them to be able to see him and he had wanted to go back to them and live through the moments of marital happiness which are the birthright of every man. But he knew now that he could not enjoy, could not really enjoy those moments he had longed for unless he did act with honor in the field.

They used to say that the first five minutes you

spent in the war were for Uncle Sam and the rest were for you. That wasn't really true, but it was true that as he saw more of it he knew that the simple issues of the war were not clearly defined in the average man's mentality. Everyone who had seen enough of it knew that with all the contradictions, the war was not being fought for the Four Freedoms; rather, that it had not been fought with too scrupulous an honesty in dealing with people like Franco and Darlan; that it was mixed up with the imperialistic struggles of the British Empire and the Russian domain. The boys had talked about this in slack moments in the hospitals. And there, in every such debate in which he had taken part, no one seriously contended that the war was a great struggle for democracy; democracy was an outmoded concept. Most of the boys agreed that the world was swinging to a totalitarian economy. That was the shape of things for which so many lives were being sacrificed. But every soldier had to achieve some individual attitude toward the war. It was a matter of personal conscience, or a debt to pay for a buddy who had been killed, or a proudness which was unwilling to tolerate cowardice on the part of the individual. And, as far as Paul Kreider was concerned, the insistence on acting like an honorable human being had come to be the basis of the war.

It was strange that Paul should reach a conception of war that was, one might say, spiritual; that from all this wreck and welter of blood and misery such a definite element of almost religious thinking should come, especially because he had never been religious. He was a young man, only twenty-five, but his thought processes had matured. He had thought of God as an ultimate power, the final cause which would not intervene to change the course of the laws of nature; that a man who depended on prayer to help solve his problems, seeking Divine intervention in his personal life, was a fool. He had thought of God as a stupendous power, the power behind the formation of space, and the explanation of the billions of light years of the universe. He had always felt this in the outdoors where he had a sense of the immensity of space and the world. That was why he loved skiing and mountain climbing when he was alone and could get up on the top of some massive slope and look out on the world which even his pygmy eyes could see; or swim far out in the ocean and feel the immensity of the plain of water.

It was strange that he had forgotten this in the mess and misery of the war, especially since he had come back to active duty from the hospital. He remembered that when he was in college—and he had done little except go to college before the war—he had told himself that whatever happened he could always try to make of his own life as much of a masterpiece as possible. Certainly there was more to the privilege of existing, even for a brief moment, than a mere adherence to the principles of Christian ethics. They had a certain function for life amongst men, but a man was a part of a larger thing than that. One had only a few seconds in the eons of time to spend on earth. Probably man was the only morsel of life conscious of itself, able to see itself with perspective. So why should one not make this moment of consciousness a thing of honor and as close to divinity as man could be?

He looked back at the pictures on the mantelpiece, the pretty girl with the baby in the old studio photograph. That might be Suzy with Dolores. But now in this moment he wanted to put them in the back of his mind so that his resolution could stay. When they would see him again, if he ever was able to get home, then they would sense a difference in him and they would know, although nothing was said about it, that he had acquitted himself with honor.

He knew suddenly, and the realization seemed to come with almost physical sharpness, that he had achieved a new definition of values—a re-definition which would give him new strength. His fear of dying seemed suddenly swept away. He had a substitute, a new code. It didn't matter so much, now, whether he was killed; the test was whether he satisfied his own conscience. He was thinking of himself, at last, as Bull had told him to do.

Paul was sure now that the only immortality, the

lasting things about this life, were honor, decency, courage, the intangibles of the spirit. Moments of bravery and honor and decency were the only permanent things in a transient world, and a man who rose to them really lived, while a man who never knew them might remain alive to the age of a hundred—and yet he never would have known the meaning of life.

As he got up from the couch the burden seemed to be lifting from his shoulders. He picked up his carbine and slung it over one arm. He started for the front door and found Jerry Bull coming in. In a second Bull's sharp blue eyes looked into Paul's and saw what he wanted to see. To Jerry, it did not matter how a man reconciled fear with his own life as long as he could live with it. How he did it was one of the secrets of his personality.

"We'll have to go up to the second platoon, Paul," he said. "The Krauts seem to be making a counter-attack. They've killed the sergeant, and it doesn't look as if White can hold them. They seem to have a couple of tanks in there."

The two walky-talky men were waiting outside. One of the radios was chattering information vital to the battle at hand. Paul listened for a moment. Then he said, "Okay, let's get up to the second platoon— and fast."

The men looked up at Paul's face as Jerry Bull had looked, and through both their minds flashed

66

the thought that the Captain h d a look almost of exaltation in his face, a glow of light in his expression. They fell in behind him and Jerry Bull as the Captain led the way swiftly along the edge of the street, heading for the sector of the second platoon.

# CHAPTER 6

IT SOUNDED AS IF ALL HELL WAS BREAKING LOOSE. This time the sounds from the front line a couple of blocks away were predominately the liquid squirts of the Schmeissers, the German burp guns. Usually the Schmeissers were in the minority because normally American fire power was superior to German in volume. When there was a German counter-attack you could almost always tell by the increase in volume of the sound of the German weapons.

This time, too, you could hear the heavy banging of artillery from the sector, perhaps our tanks or the German tanks or self-propelled guns which had been reported involved in the counter-attack. You could hear the cracking of the cannons as they were fired, the short screech through the air as the shells flew toward their targets, and the explosion. That combination meant that a short-range weapon was being fired with a flat trajectory. That sequence of the closely spaced report of the gun, the short interval of flight and the immediate explosion indicated tanks or SP's.

This time Paul Kreider didn't duck as he heard them coming and landing a couple of blocks away.

He was sure now that he would be able to take it. In fact, he would be able to ride on the platoons just as Colonel Tom had ordered. Paul told his walky-talky operator connecting with battalion to inform headquarters that he was going up to the second platoon. He heard the operator repeating the code words, "Dog Easy Vistor to Dog Tare: I am going up to second stall; I am going up to second stall. Bogies are coming in there; Bogies are coming in there."

Things seemed to be happening fast. The Germans were making a counter-attack against C Company, on his right, too. Paul could hear the calls coming in from Captain Carey, the CO of the company. Evidently it was a good-sized effort to push back the American attack.

Paul, Colonel Bull and the two radio men rounded a corner and reached the platoon headquarters, but the place was deserted. The sound-power line of the telephone, however, had been extended beyond and they trailed it down another street. Paul was watching the windows carefully and trying to avoid a wrong turn, and his mind was working clearly. He kept his eyes moving and his progress was swift. He told Bull to watch the left side of the street as they progressed, while he took the right. But there was no movement in the windows.

Suddenly they reached a street corner where the sounds of firing grew loud and insistent. The sound-power line wound up the front steps of a stone house and they followed. They knew then that they were within a stone's throw of the crux of the action.

Inside the house they found White sitting on the bottom step of the stairway, feverishly writing out a message on his yellow message pad. The Lieutenant's face lit up as he saw help coming. "We're having a hell of a time, Captain," he said. "The Krauts seem to have about two platoons of infantry down there and a couple of SP guns. I've got the men out on a skirmish line trying to hold them. I don't know how the hell we're going to get to our objective today, no matter how much the big shot wants to be there. It's going to be all we can do to hang on to what we've got. I was just sending back a message to you asking if we can get some help up here, maybe an extra tank or an extra mortar squad."

Paul felt that his brain was working efficiently as it used to in his first days in the field. "Okay, okay, we'll get up some extra stuff, but first let me go up and take a look at what's going on. Meanwhile, we'll pull a couple of tanks from the first platoon to help out." He took the message pad, ripped off the sheet which Lieutenant White had started and began another message. "Have you got a runner here?" he asked as he was writing.

White called one. Paul stuffed the carbon in his pocket and gave the message to the runner. "Do you

71

know where the first platoon is?" he asked the runner.

"I think so, sir."

"Well, run on over with this and if you can't find
them, go on back to company headquarters and ask
for Thorson, my company runner." Then Paul said,
thinking quickly, "No, never mind going back to
company headquarters. You just find first platoon
headquarters." And he took his map case and pointed
out the place where the platoon headquarters would
probably be located. He was thinking that if the al-
ternative of going back to company headquarters
were presented, the runner would undoubtedly go
there, finding an excuse to take a breather from the
dangerous sector of the second platoon. Paul grinned
as he thought about it, because, he told himself, a
few minutes before he would have jumped at the
same opportunity.

"You'd better come on up with us," Paul said to
White, "and we'll take a look at this thing."

He watched a shadow of apprehension pass swiftly over White's face. Paul knew that not so long ago
he would have reacted that way, but now he seemed
calm or as nearly calm as one could be under the circumstances.

Outside, the sounds of battle were growing increasingly intense and loud. It seemed as if the fight
must be right around the corner. You could hear
single rifle shots almost as loudly as if you were fir-

ing them yourself. "This is going to be tough," he told himself.

They followed White. White was not one to stick his neck out by traveling in the open, along the streets. So this time they went through the back door of the house into a little courtyard and up by a ladder to the top of the roof, across the roof and beyond over a wall topped with broken glass. There was a schoolyard with a playground beyond. They crossed the playground and White waved them to a stop. "Hold it," he said. He was muttering something about someone being there. He was obviously looking around for some members of one of his squads when the squirt of a burp gun practically on top of them snapped in their ears. Paul saw something smack into the wall near White, and all of them jumped to the opposite side of the alley. The sounds of the "papercutters" had come from the end of the alley on the right side somewhere. Then they saw two doughfoots, ahead in the open street, crouching behind a pile of raked debris from an old air raid. It was evidently toward them that the sniper was directing his fire.

White, in the lee of the protecting wall, motioned the men to come back from their exposed position. Paul watched them glancing fearfully in the direction of the sniper, waiting their chance, and then jumping up and dashing for the alley. They made it. They were out of breath and scared. White spoke in low tones. "Where's the rest of the squad?" he wanted to know. One of the men, his eyes haunted by fear, said, "I don't know. We got separated when the Krauts came in. There's a tank around here some place. We can hear the motor. That rattly sound. I think some of the squad got hurt."

"We were up in the next street," said the other. Two or three got killed. I think we're the only ones left. We're trying to hold this sector, sir."

Paul knew that the man was overstating the case, but that the squad had been disorganized and the Germans were evidently out in some force. The problem was to find the pieces of the squad and hold it until our tanks and a bazooka crew could get up and take care of the counter-attack. He asked the men, "Where did you last see the others?"

The haunted eyes turned toward him. The man had to shout because the burp gunner around the corner let go another squirt. "It's down that street." And he pointed to the wide avenue at the end of the alley.

It would be dangerous to go out into the open with the burp gunners firing. Paul needed more information. Now that he had secured control of his emotions, although even now he was not without fear, he found he could think clearly once more. Usually the accelerated tempo and excitement of action lead to a quickness of decision and sometimes a pace that is too swift, but this time he was able to work out the steps without inefficiency. The fog had lifted from his consciousness.

"Do you mean the house on the other side of the street?" he asked the enlisted man. "Is that where you saw the squad last?"

"Yes, sir. We were spread out along the front yard when the thing began. The Krauts let a couple of shells go from their tank and we scattered out. We were afraid the tank would come down the street and we didn't have any bazooka team."

Well, then, thought Paul, the remnants of the squad must be stretched along the other side of the street, probably in the sunken enclosures around the cellar windows.

"What happened to the wounded?" he asked the other man.

"I don't know, sir, but I think two of them was killed."

Paul knew his enlisted men well enough to be aware that first reports were always the worst. Now there was only one thing to do, and that was to find out the truth of the situation. Cautiously Paul worked his way along the wall to a position near the street where he might be able to see how the other members of the squad were disposed, and how bad the situation really was. Obviously the two men were in no condition to give an account of it.

It was a long ten or twelve feet he had to traverse to get to the end of the alley, opening on the street;

75

especially because he wasn't sure from just which angle the snipers were firing. He drew closer, carefully. A cascade of sound was coming from the right. Mostly the sounds were German Schmeissers, but this time there were a few reports of American M-1 rifles. That meant there were some of his squad up there. He knew then that he would have to reconnoiter to the right rather than the left. If he could only get across the street he would have a good view from behind the pile of rubble on the small lawn of the house on the other side. To get there he would have to dash, fast and unexpectedly—as one must always do when a field of fire is covered by enemy weapons.

It was an old knack learned through experience, but the hardest part was always the moment when you decided to begin to run. When the firing slackened he tensed himself for the effort, jumped up and ran bent at the waist across the open part of the street. Just as he reached the other side he heard a long burst of sniper fire from the righthand side, heard the bullets crack through the air. But he dove for the pile of rubble, sliding into the ground with the mound between him and the unseen marksman. The German sniper had missed.

There was an indentation in the wall of houses beyond the pile of rubble—a corner where one house sat farther back than the others in the row. If he could reach that corner he might get a better look down the street. He waited a short time, counting the seconds. Then, tensing his muscles like a sprinter, made the final dash—a distance of five or six yards. This time the German didn't fire until a fraction of a second after he reached shelter.

As he hugged the edge of the brick building, four or five German burp guns opened up on him at once. This, he thought, must be the street along which the counter-attack had been progressing. The counter-attack was probably a squad of Germans trying to push down the avenue and get in behind the platoon, but it was certain that there were still some of the members of his squad holding up the Krauts farther down the street.

Paul looked up at the six or seven windows of the house beside which he crouched. They were bare and expressionless, without glass. Inside, one could see broken beams and boards and furniture. If he could get up to one of those windows and if there were no Germans in the house, perhaps he could get a good look down the length of the street. If those snipers didn't spot him.

He decided to do that, to get up the front stairs to a window. If he stayed well back from the window he wouldn't be too good a target. He moved cautiously along the wall of the building. Then he ran up the steps and through the front door.

Inside, the stairs were almost intact, carpeted, covered with dirt and dust. He reached the second

77

story, stumbled into a bedroom. The ceiling was a tangle of lath and a patch of sky. But the window embrasure seemed quite untouched, dark and secure. He stood well back from it beside a bureau and found to his delight that he commanded a good view of the street. He was also delighted to see four out-stretched figures in American OD down there, disposed along a low wall at the street corner. Just a few feet behind them, between them and him, were two more brown-clad figures: one sprawled behind a fallen cornice; the other, across the street, crouched behind a front porch. All seemed to be alive, un-hurt; for they held their rifles at the alert.

As he watched, he saw flashes come from two or three rifles. And from somewhere down the street again came the sounds of German "papercutters." He couldn't see the Germans. They were good at concealment, being good soldiers. But he knew that if he looked sharply he might be able to spot some hostile movement in one of the buildings in the next block. And because of his position high up in the house, it was possible he could spot such a move-ment better than someone on the ground.

At any rate, he had found a larger part of the squad; only two men unaccounted for. And as far as he could see, the ragged skirmish line of six men strung out along the block seemed to be holding the Germans pretty well.

He was just thinking that, when he heard the

sound. It was a whistling and rattling sound and he knew it instantly: a German tank engine, farther down the block. The German scouts had evidently decided there was no American tank in the vicinity so they were going to run out their vehicle and finish off the remnants of the infantry squad while they were pinned down by the German fire. Then he saw the tank snap into sight around the corner two blocks away; it was lurching, jerking. It trailed a belch of violet-colored smoke. It was a Mark IV with a long-barreled 77 gun.

He saw the group of four doughfoots closest to the tank lying still as stones, while the creature lurched around the corner and straightened into the length of the street and hesitated for a moment. Then the engine raced and roared again. The tank lunged forward, began to roll toward the doughboys.

Then he saw them move. The tank was no more than fifty feet away, and it would be only a matter of a few seconds before it saw them and would strew them with machine-gun fire. He knew there was no bazooka team with the squad. And so he wasn't surprised when he saw one of the brown-clad fig-ures grabbing for a hand grenade. He saw the arm move in that awkward stiff motion, saw the pill fly toward the tank, bounce off and explode. Almost the same second the other arms tossed grenades, and a cloud of sudden smoke covered the area around the tank. Still from the cloud of smoke and dust and settling debris the tank nudged forward at increasing speed. The secret was now out; the tank men knew that Americans were within grenade range. If they were sharp-eyed, the Germans had probably seen the pine-apples sailing through the air toward the tank.

The tank was virtually on top of the four men when two more grenades broke in front of it, spattering it with fragments. But the defense was hopeless. In the excitement of the moment two of the doughfoots leaped to their feet and began to run. Paul saw the flat steel turret turn, saw the machine-gun barrel swivel, and watched the tracers flying around the two running forms of men. One of them fell with the first burst. The other ran around ten yards before he was caught in his tracks, spun around and sprawled out on the pavement.

The tank lumbered on, clattering over the street surface, bumping over the piles of bricks, and apparently failing to notice the other two forms of soldiers lying near the path. Now he saw the tank coming almost straight for him, and it seemed inevitable that it would pass directly beneath the house. He pulled back from the window to avoid being seen. There was no point in watching the tank and exposing himself unless he was going to do something about it.

If he only had a bazooka team here! The grinding and rattling of the engine of war grew louder

80

until it seemed as if it must be in the front yard; that it couldn't be closer. He heard the engine rev down a little. Then he heard the tank's machine guns fire, and heard the clatter of bullets zipping into the windows of the first story of the house.. Probably one of the tank men had detected some movement, and the tank, following the usual procedure, was spraying all the windows in the vicinity to make sure no American was being overlooked.

It was then that Paul decided to do it. He thought of his own hand grenades. He had two, just as everyone carried two or three, in his musette bag. If the tank was stopped ouside the window he could perhaps drop a grenade squarely on the grill above the engine. He knew that many of the carcasses of burned-out tanks which he had seen littering the sides of the road had been set afire by strafing American planes. This was done by direct hits of incendiary bullets landing in the open cowl on the top of the tank chassis, the ventilating grill above the engine compartment.

If only he had a thermite grenade! He felt in the musette bag to see. If he remembered, there were a thermite grenade and a concussion grenade. He found these handy for clearing out cellars where recalcitrant Germans might be hiding. As his hands struck the inside of the knapsack he felt the smooth surface of the therm te grenade.

Those weie long steps between the point where he

81

was standing and the window. Each one must have been a mile long, and each one seemed to last an eternity. But the longest time of all was the moment of decision before he made the first step. For just a second he thought about letting the tank go by and hurrying back to get up a bazooka squad. Perhaps that would have been the sensible thing to do. But he thought of the whole first squad pinned now between the tank and the German lines, and the second platoon headquarters which lay almost directly in the path of the German armored vehicle, if the vehicle should choose to penetrate that far into the American positions.

That was why he made that first step and the others which came afterward—that and the fact that on the other side of the street Jerry Bull was watching. In a fraction of a second he was at the window and quickly he saw that he was not going to be able to drop the grenade with accuracy unless he climbed out on the roof, for the tank was beyond the house and a gable barred direct vision. He leaned out as far as he could, then quickly climbed out onto the gable roof and worked his way along the slate covering, hoping that the tank gunner would not turn his turret in that direction and spot him.

Those were probably the most harrowing moments he ever spent, edging his way across the slates, clinging to the metal rain gutter with his toes, making one step at a time sideways, with his body stretched out across the slope of the roof. And then he found himself directly over the square, ugly brown shape of the Mark IV. A thrill coursed through his scalp as he saw the grate over the engine, the black opening through which air was allowed to enter. He turned partly toward the tank, his heels braced against the gutter underneath the roof's edge. Then he straightened up almost to a sitting position, fished out the thermite grenade and pulled the pin. He knew that there would be a four-second delay. He would have to hold it about two seconds, so that it would explode at about the same instant it struck the grill. Should take about two seconds for the missle to fall. Then, if he had timed it right, some of the fragments of burning thermite might penetrate the grill and ignite the gasoline fumes in the engine hatch. It was worth the chance.

Then he laughed to himself. It was funny to be sprawling on the roof of a house in a German city with a German tank sitting right under you, thermite grenade in one hand and the fuse burning down, while across the street your old friend from Newton High School was watching you.

As he was thinking this and grinning to himself the German riflemen down the length of the street spotted him. He heard the cracking of their rifles and the short burst of Schmeisser fire and saw the chunks of slate flying from the roof beyond him. It was time to drop the grenade. He let it go and in almost the same instant flung his body over to the right as the German snipers peppered the spot where he had been sprawled. In an instant he heard the "pop" of the thermite grenade below, and he hoped for a bigger explosion as he scrambled madly for the window. He reached the window which, being indented from direct range of vision, was not an easy target for the German marksmen. He fell through the aperture and onto the dust-covered floor just as he heard the roaring explosion outside the house. The force of the explosion blew in the window sash and pieces of it fell on top of him. He was really grinning as he jumped up and ran for the stairs. In the confusion he might be able to get back to the other side of the street. As he came down the stairs another explosion shook the air and he heard another burst of firing outside. Bullets flew into the front windows and his heart sank. His mind raced: those Krauts have come down the street and they've got me hemmed in. He fell to the floor and crawled toward the window at the side of the house. Perhaps he could make his exit there. Another fusilade of firing zipped through the window at the front just as he reached the portico.

It was a low window. He dragged himself over the sill and swung a leg down the side of the house. For a moment he dangled by his hands, then dropped. He hit the pavement and rolled. He found himself in another one of those alleyways between

84

houses. This one led to the street, and he thought immediately that if he could make the street while the Germans stormed the house, as they undoubtedly would, then he could possibly take advantage of tactical surprise to make a break for the other side of the road.

He hurried along the wall until he was only a foot or so from the little lawn in front of the house. There was another pile of brick in the alley at this point. He sprawled behind it, lifted his head cautiously above the top. What he saw was startling. The body of a German panzer trooper lay in the middle of the pavement, and across the road, standing in the alley, feet widespread, was Jerry Bull with his carbine at ready. It had been Bull and the two-walky-talky men with the aid of the remaining members of the first squad who had been firing into the windows of the house, he almost immediately realized. The firing into the windows had been only an incidental result of a heavy fusilade directed toward the tank. He knew then that he had made a bull's-eye with the thermite grenade, set the tank afire, and that the Germans had tried to unbutton their burning vehicle and escape.

As he watched, he became aware that Bull was motioning to someone in the direction of the tank, pointing his carbine in the same direction. Probably it was a surviving member of the tank crew who wanted to surrender, although Paul did not choose to expose himself by stepping out to see what might be left of the German panzer vehicle. He could restrain his curiosity until he reached to the other side of the street. No use risking being shot in the back by the Germans farther down the avenue for the sake of a mere look at a destroyed Mark IV.

Now he saw that Bull was apparently being successful in inducing the German tanker to come over and surrender. In a second Paul saw the figure of the German, clad in the special gray-green uniform of the panzer troops, shambling toward Jerry with hands over his head and a white handkerchief dangling from one fist.

Bull beckoned the German into the alley and stood back at a half crouch, while two of the men took the German's pistol belt and knife from his waist. They shoved him flat against the wall and went through his pockets while Jerry Bull covered him with a carbine.

In the lull in the firing Paul heard the heavy clumping of feet running down the street, and in a second saw two of the men who had been strung out farther down the street, run back into the alley. They were probably the two who had lain doggo while the tank passed, when the other two were killed. There were two more doughfoots on the other side of the street farther up toward the corner— the ones he had seen from the window. And Paul was thinking: if I could only get a machine gun-squad up here, I could straighten out this situation; that and a bazooka team, in case another Kraut tank shows up. But first I'll have to get across the street so I can get some instructions back to platoon head-quarters—if I can make it.

He was awaiting his chance when he heard a distinct pinging sound, coming from the direction of the Germans. It was a mortar. He had an instantaneous reaction to hit the ground. You couldn't hear a mortar shell approaching. Paul by training and experience was a good enough soldier to know that. So he was hugging the ground when the projectile struck. It landed somewhere near the street corner, with a violent explosion. He thought: if they have any observation they will probably drop the next one a little closer to where I am.

And so it happened. The mortar shell landed between him and the Germans, and he took advantage of the flying debris and smoke and dust to dash across the open street. This time the Germans were off guard. They did not fire at him with small arms. He reached the other side of the street; reached the alley safely and found Bull guarding the German prisoner, with the remnants of the first squad beside him. The remnants, that is, except for the two men still pinned down in the street. He thought about the necessity of sending back a messenger asking for a bazooka team and machine-gun squad, and saw that Jerry Bull was smiling and saying,

"Nice work, kid!" Then Paul laughed; in his hurry to get across the street, he hadn't even stopped to glance at the wreckage of the German tank he had destroyed.

# CHAPTER 7

THE PROBLEM NOW WAS TO GET THOSE TWO REMAIN-
ing men back from their advance position near the
street corner. Then the remnants of the squad could
be used as a unit and spread out in a skirmish line,
to hold until the machine-gun squad and the bazooka team could come up to deal with the German
counter-attack. Every moment was precious because
at any time the Germans might make a determined
push. In their present position, the first squad would
have a hard time holding the Krauts, or preventing
their breaking through to platoon headquarters.
Furthermore, if Paul didn't get the last two men out
of the street corner pretty quickly they would probably be hurt by the mortars the Germans were beginning to fire into the vicinity. He thought of the
practical expedient of shouting and decided to do
just that.

The other four members of the squad knew the
names of those in the street. Paul learned them and
began to call: "Johnson and Bildad! Come back
here!" He repeated the call. At the same time, he
noticed that the German prisoner, at first stunned

and shocked, seemed to be regaining his equilibrium. He was a narrow-eyed, short, dark-complexioned man. Paul could read the changes going on in the German's mind; he knew the Teutonic mentality; he could follow the German's shift from fear to apathy, then to a state almost of defiance. Probably the Kraut was thinking: "If I had known there were so few Americans, I might not have been so anxious to surrender." Paul watched him for a second and then he forgot about the German as Johnson and Bildad clumped down the street and slid into the alleyway.

Now six of the members of the first squad were reunited, including the corporal, Bildad. Paul instructed Bildad, glancing at his map, "Better take three men around to the other side of the street and work along that alley. You can get clear through the block and find the third platoon flank."

One of the men was a Browning Automatic rifleman. Paul said, "You can stick your BAR man out on the left flank where he'll have some fire power, in case the Krauts try to get through the street. I'd keep two more on the corner in that alley right over there. Better stretch out the other two on this side of the street, watching that corner down there. Maybe you can get one of them up on top of the school building to make sure the Krauts don't try to get across the intersection, and we'll get you a machine-gun squad and a bazooka team up here to help out.

I'll send you a runner to make sure your messages get back to platoon headquarters."

As he was speaking he heard the ping of another mortar. They all ducked and the projectile crashed into the street at the corner. Jerry Bull said, "As long as they don't get off the street with their mortar fire, we'll be okay." Then he nodded his head toward the German prisoner and said to Paul, "What do you propose to do with this jerk?"

Paul said, "You and I are going to take him back to platoon headquarters and let them work on him. Then we can get up the bazooka team and the machine-gun squad they need here." He went on, "What's been going on with the walky-talkies?"

"I don't know. You've been making so goddamn much noise on the other side of the street, I couldn't hear anything." He and Jerry laughed, but they had to duck in a second when a mortar shell crashed without warning into the top of the school building, spraying fragments of roofing and drain pipe into the alley. It was time to move and Paul felt his nerves shaking a little as every man's nerves must shake when potential death strikes close. Still he found that a new steadiness, a negative quality called courage kept him efficient.

"Bildad, better get your men spread out before they get hurt," he said. Then he nodded toward the prisoner and said to Jerry Bull, "Will you watch that character? I'll lead the way."

They started back. They had to cross the little school yard beyond the alley. It was relatively open but probably none of them thought of it as dangerous. It was only a few yards of open space before you reached another alley.

Paul started across, with the walky-talky men prodding the prisoner; then sad little White and Jerry bringing up the rear. Paul had nearly reached the wall on the other side of the school yard when he heard the clap of a rifle from the German side of town. A single shot. There was a gasping sound behind him, a choking sob, and snapping his body around Paul saw the others breaking for cover; saw Jerry Bull hit the pavement, and noticed that Jerry fell particularly limp.

Then Paul knew that Bull was hurt. The compact form of the paratrooper lay flat, still in a direct field of fire of the German sniper. There was no telling when the German marksman would shoot again. Paul yelled to the walky-talky men, "Cover the prisoner" —and jumped toward Jerry. He tried to lift his friend. Then he saw that Bull's head lolled on his neck and his face had suddenly become ashen gray. A dark-red, wet stain covered his chest.

Paul dragged him to the lee of the wall, safe from the German sniper; there he sat him up against the stone. Jerry was dead. There was no denying that. His face was masklike. The jaw sagged loosely.

92

Jerry's jacket had been ripped. Paul tore it apart and saw the oozing blood, the round hole.

Then Paul turned on the German—to him the personification of the force they were fighting, the individual who stood for the German Army.

A black mist flooded over Paul, and the German cowered, his face twisted with terror.

Paul had a carbine. Why didn't he use it? He picked it up, snarling at the German and leveling it, "Now you're going to get yours!"

The rage had become overpowering. Paul could hardly see the German. He clicked off the safety of his carbine. The German was becoming hysterical. He was shouting, "No, no, I didn't, I couldn't," in English, and repeating himself.

Then the black mist began to fade and Paul's finger didn't touch the trigger. The same forces of restraint which had held back the instinct of cowardliness were holding him now. If he hadn't had the litttle talk with himself this morning in the house, if he hadn't settled on basic reasons for keeping on with the struggle, then he would have killed the German on the spot.

He lowered his rifle. It was not right to kill an unarmed man in cold blood. The fact that the enemy had done that in many cases didn't make it any more right or honorable. If we were going to repay treatment in kind, then there was no point in fighting the war. We could use force just as effectively as,

93

and in most cases much more effectively than the Germans. But we could do the job coldly and efficiently and justly. Paul said to the German, "You son-of-a-bitch, I'm going to let the M.P.'s take care of you."

Then he prodded him into a standing position while the German was slobbering, "Thank you, thank you." And Paul told him to get going before he changed his mind.

There was nothing more to do about his best friend, Jerry Bull. The paratrooper, propped up against the wall, sat still, massive, very lifeless: a thing, an image of a man, no longer a human being. No good in talking to that inanimate object; the person who had been Jerry Bull was gone.

There was urgent business to attend to. He still had to get back to the second platoon headquarters to send up a bazooka team. He'd have to make sure that a machine-gun squad would get up to the area under stress. Paul and the others started back over the rooftops and through the hallways and then into the silent streets.

Back at platoon headquarters he found out that the machine-gun squad was already on the way up. He got together the litter squad and sent it up to get Jerry's body. The least he could do was to carry away the mortal remains, so that they could be decently buried.

He called company headquarters on the phone and told Thorson to send over a bazooka team from the first platoon. The bazooka team came in from the first platoon and he went forward with the team, the walky-talky men, and shocked, sad little Lieutenant White following. They moved up toward the sector of the counter-attack.

Working their way along the street, they passed the litter squad carrying the heavy burden. Bodies always had that inert, weighted look. Paul stared for a moment, then quickly turned his face away.

A block from the front they could hear a loud and tumultuous spasm of firing. The Germans must be trying the break through the skirmish line of the squad: so, for the last block, they ran, not only to get there in time, but also because they couldn't tell just where the attack was coming or whether they might run into Germans at the next corner— and in that case, it was better to be in motion.

As they ran, Paul was thinking of Jerry Bull. Seeing his friend killed with such suddenness had stirred up some of the doubts and fears he had known before. But it was only a passing flash of thought, for the Germans were moving in.

Clearly Paul could hear the burping sound of several Schmeissers and the crash of mortar shells. This sounded like a real attempt at a break. They skirted the main street, swinging through the alley they had followed before, over the roof of the garage and through the school, to find Corporal Bildad crouching at the end of the narrow corridor, firing his carbine down the street. As he saw them, he shouted back, "They're getting in closer. They seem to be coming over the roofs in the next block. My BAR man got hurt and they may be able to get around my left flank."

It was always like this. You could never be sure just where the enemy was or how he was operating, any more than he could be sure of your movements. Part of the game was to keep under cover and the battlefield almost always—apparently, at least—was deserted, except by those sounds of almost mysterious origin. But Paul knew that if he made a dash into the open, the air over the street would be peopled with the cracking sounds of bullets and the Schmeissers would be rattling from their unseen perches in the next block. It was worth a chance. If the flank crumpled, he would be in a bad spot.

"Where is the machine-gun squad going to set up?" he asked Bildad.

"I think out on the left flank where the Krauts seem to be pushing hardest," Bildad said. "I've already got them across the street."

"Good," said Paul. "But I think we ought to get that BAR out of there; then we can use it some other place. Have you been able to do anything about that mortar?"

"No, sir, we haven't been able to find him, but he hasn't been firing for the last few minutes."

"Well," Paul said, "you better get a man on the other side of the street and get that BAR man out of there and get the weapon back here. We can use it."

Just then he heard the heavy bap! bap! bap! of an American machine gun close by. "That's good," he said. "The squad is in position."

There was one more thing he'd have to do. He'd have to get a tank up into this sector to give some reinforcement in case the German armor showed up. Just for his own satisfaction he moved up to the edge of the alley and took a look at the wreckage of the burned-out Mark IV which he had destroyed a few minutes before. It was burned a salmon-pink color and a charred body was draped over the top of the turret in front of the opened hatch.

"Are the Krauts trying to rush you?" he asked Corporal Bildad. Bildad said, "No, but they've been firing so much that it looks as if they might try."

"Is there any place where you can see the street from around here?" he asked Bildad.

"The best place I know is that house across the street where you were when you threw the grenade, Captain," Bildad said.

Paul thought: it looks as if I'll have to get back up there to get a look. But maybe going up again will be tempting fate.

The Germans were firing again in considerable

volume and the American machine gun on the left flank of the squad's position was tacking away vigorously. You could hear single shots of the M-1's from the vicinity where the Americans were sniping at windows in the next block. It was the usual hit-or-miss business of street fighting, where you fire a lot of bullets in the hope that something will be hit. Then Paul heard Corporal Bildad say softly, "I see the son-of-a-bitch. I see him moving." He had been craning his neck around the corner, trying to see what was happening and had evidently spotted a German. He fired his carbine two or three times, but the German fired back. The bullets bounced off the street surface as Bildad recoiled.

"I think they're coming down the street," he said. "I saw that one get up and run." Then they all jumped as they heard the sudden angry snarl of the burp gun right on top of them somewhere to the right. It sounded as if the gun was in the school building, and the bullets bounced off the back wall of the alley.

Bildad whispered, "He's in the school building. I'm going in." And he started down the alley, keeping to the side least exposed to view from the school building.

Meanwhile a fusilade of shots rang out in the street. The men of the squad disposed on both sides were pouring out a volume of M-1 fire, and the Germans were matching them, shot for shot. You

98

could tell when a German moved, because there would be a sudden smother of American shots. Yes, this was it. This was the counter-attack they had expected.

# CHAPTER 8

IN A SECOND THEY HEARD ANOTHER SCHMEISSER CRACK-ling from behind them. The Germans had infiltrated clear around their position. It was easy to understand how it could have happened, with so little outpost security. The bullets clipped into the walls on both sides of the alley and, with a rush, Paul, the two walky-talky men, White and Bildad dove out of the narrow passageway into the courtyard of the school building. As Paul hit the ground he saw Bildad fall and roll over on one side. They had done the wrong thing in jumping into the school yard, with the Germans probably hiding in the school building.

Paul jumped up and dashed for the lee of the garage as the Schmeissers continued to snarl, following him across the open space. Now the flank was really exposed. Unless he could pull the first platoon flank farther over to close up the gap he might have to contend with a deep German penetration. Right now, however, there was only one thing to do, and that was to get under cover. They got to the garage and flopped behind one of the neatly piled collections of rubble which could be seen all over Unterbach.

Bildad had it bad, that was sure. He hadn't been able to move from the place where he fell and rolled over. And the bullets were whacking into the ground around him. As Paul watched, a bullet smacked squarely into the prostrate body and kicked it over —and the bullets still came.

Paul was looking for those bastardly Germans. Somewhere in the vicinity they were watching and firing. If he could only spot them! He looked quickly up at the upper stories of the building, around him, searching for a sign of the marksmen who were firing at Bildad. And then he saw it: he saw the dark form behind a window opening on the third floor of the school building, saw the head moving and the little puffs of smoke coming out of the blunt snout of the barrel a couple of inches inside the window. In a second he had whipped out his carbine, snapping off the safety and let one go; too fast. The German stopped firing and the form pulled out of the shadow, leaving it blank.

You could never tell when you hit a man, but Paul knew it wasn't a good shot. He should have been more thorough than that. He cursed himself for hurrying, and looked around for the other Germans in the vicinity. Two or three must be between his position and the second platoon headquarters. These would have to be cleaned out, but there were still more around. The question was whether or not they had been able to infiltrate in any number through the skirmish line; whether the men holding the skirmish line farther up were still in position. He would have to see.

But now that he had to stick his neck out again his old malady was returning. Something that seemed to be logic was telling him to go back to platoon headquarters and try to reorganize the broken skirmish line from there. Wasn't it logical that there he could co-ordinate the other platoons and close them in on the flanks and seal off the break? From there, too, he would be able to find out what happened to our tanks, why they didn't come up, and he would also be able to report direct by telephone to battalion headquarters. You could never depend on these walky-talkies. Maybe he was talking himself into this, but it was certainly White's job to run the platoon; a captain had to manage his company. It wasn't the place of a captain to stay up with a squad. He was supposed to exercise a command function; how could he co-ordinate platoons unless he was in the right place, and in communication with the troops under his command? Yes, he had better move quickly before the situation got out of control, and he had better leave to Lieutenant White the first squad with its broken skirmish line. But he would have to move fast if he was to get out of here, to get past the Germans who had swung around the flank of the squad's position.

He told the walky-talky men, "We've got to get back to platoon headquarters quickly." They, being as scared as he, quickly got to their feet and followed as he struck down the alley, dashed across the open space, reached the garage and climbed up on the roof, ran across the flat surface and hoped that the German in the school building had not taken up a new post in one of the windows. He climbed the iron fence, went through the hallway, and came into the open street, looking up and down cautiously, for the Germans might conceivably have penetrated this far and retaken some of the houses they had previously vacated.

When he got to platoon headquarters he grabbed the sound-power phone and called company headquarters. Thorson answered the phone. He told Thorson, "See if you can get the other platoons. I can't get them from here. I want you to tell Milo, Lieutenant Milo and Lieutenant Perrine at first and third platoons to close in the flanks; we are being overrun in the second platoon sector. Estimate about a platoon of Krauts. And tell the heavy-weapons headquarters to get another machine-gun squad up to the second platoon pronto."

From the sector under stress the sounds of battle continued. He could hear firing: the snarling sound of the Schmeissers and the blasting sound of a mortar or bazooka. He hoped it was the explosion of bazooka shells he was hearing and not German mortar shells. If he could only hurry this thing up and get the people in the line! He'd better not go on up to the first squad again, despite the confusion there, but back to company headquarters. The pseudo-logic which drives men rearwards was convincing him, "If I could get back to company CP, I could probably check on the whole deal and speed it up; besides, Thorson might be drunk. Didn't think of that. He might screw up the deal. It would be better if I went on back. Besides, I could check on the situation of the other platoons and see if they are pushing along." So he said to the radio men, "Let's go on back to company headquarters."

The company headquarters was still in the building across the street from the bank, the one with the smashed-in roof and the puddle of water in the middle of the rug underneath the telephone.

Thorson was on the phone, not drunk, and surprised to see him so soon. "Sounds like a godawful battle you're having up there, Captain," he said.

In a moment Captain Kreider felt the pride which comes when people behind the lines say, "Quite a battle *you're* having up there," as if the other person were an admiring outsider and *you* were in the fraternity.

In the same moment Paul felt a twinge of remorse because the logic which had supported his retreat began to ring false. He was ashamed, for he realized now that he could have controlled the whole show from the sector under stress, and he was aware that he had left the first squad in a very serious moment without even a squad leader, and without even deputizing a squad leader. Goddamn it, he thought, if White weren't such a milk-and-water character I could leave it with him. Why do I, a captain, have to go around leading a squad? That should be White's job. But logic emerging slowly from the stress and strain of fear told him that it was the captain's responsibility to see that all the weak points in the line were stopped; that, as the *Officers' Guide,* which he had studied so religiously in his younger days as a second lieutenant, put it: "The company commander is responsible for the execution of all activities pertaining to the unit."

Even if White's weakness was responsible for the collapse of a sector, Paul was, in the last analysis, the final source of responsibility.

He would have to go back to the second platoon and hold that tottering organization together. First, he would have to check on the other platoons, however, and see whether there were any new developments. "How is the push going in the other platoon sectors? he asked Sergeant Humphries.

"Okay, sir," said the Sergeant. Humphries seemed to have recovered some of his lost respect for his commanding officer, for he knew that this morning

106

Paul had been riding the platoons, and even the squads.

Paul called battalion on the phone. "Colonel Tom? I've got a counter-attack about platoon strength, I'd say, in the second-platoon sector. They had a tank, at least one. We knocked it out. I'm trying to pull in my flanking platoons and cover up the gap. The first squad lost five men. I've sent up a bazooka team and machine-gun squad from the heavy-weapons company to beef it up."

"Can you handle it?" Colonel Tom's tired voice rasped into the receiver.

"Yes, sir, I think I can close it off all right."

Colonel Tom paused, then said, "Have you been up there?"

"Yes, sir, I just got back."

"Well, I want you to ride on it so we can straighten it out and get going. We've had another call from Division saying they want us to get to Phase Line D today, and you'll have to get this thing straightened out before we can go on."

Paul was furious. This was another accusation of neglect of duty and it was unwarranted. Angry, insubordinate words struggled for utterance. He wanted to blow off steam, to tell about the German tank, to tell how he had been working with the squads.

But he thought better of it. He said, "Yes, sir," and hung up. And he realized he had been off base.

He was thinking: I shouldn't be back here in company headquarters now. No wonder the Colonel is upset. There shouldn't have been any counter-attack anyway with the Krauts out there in such small strength. If I had been on the ball I would have held the thing together instead of screwing back here to sit on my behind at company headquarters.

Then he thought, Kreider, what am I going to do with you? You're always flunking out at the critical moment. I thought you had it all straightened out. Now you're acting like a dog. You left White in the lurch and you've screwed up the whole second platoon.

He was still reviling himself as he got up from the table. "Kreider, I'm going to kick your tail right up to the second platoon and straighten out this goddamn mess before you finally convince yourself that you're a jerk."

He told the walky-talky men, "Let's get moving. We're going back up to the second platoon."

# CHAPTER 9

Paul ran most of the way, dogtrotting down the ruined streets, with the two walky-talky men following him. He had a bullet in the chamber of his carbine, but the safety was on. He held the gun at the ready as he ran, because it was possible that the Krauts might have penetrated through the second platoon position if they had realized their degree of success. At once the bad and the good thing about war, depending on which side you were on, was that usually you didn't know how successful you had been until too late to make the most of it.

He listened for the sounds of the battle ahead as he ran, thinking that it was strangely silent up there. He was within a block of platoon headquarters and he was wondering whether the silence was a good or bad omen. Perhaps the Germans had wiped out the first squad and were pushing forward to new positions. Perhaps the German noncoms were getting their men together to make another push, or perhaps they had gone even one step beyond and were spreading them out at various points in the advancing skirmish line.

He found the answer when he got to the second platoon headquarters. Miraculously, the Germans had been driven back and the lost ground regained. Lieutenant White, the platoon sergeant told him, had stayed up with the squad to straighten it out. He had sent a runner back to report that the situation was under control.

Paul traversed the two blocks between platoon headquarters and the school building at a quick walk. He moved carefully through the hallway, over the iron gate and the top of the garage, watching zealously for any sign of movement in the windows —for although White had reported the trouble cleared up, one could never be sure. He reached the alley near the burned-out tank and discovered Lieutenant White with two or three of the squad members standing beside him, caring for the prostrate and almost lifeless Corporal Bildad.

Paul looked into White's face and thought he saw a new look of steadiness there. He also sensed something of resentment in White's attitude toward him. After all, he had left the squad in the lurch, hadn't he? And he had left Corporal Bildad to the mercy of the infiltrating German riflemen.

"How did you get it straightened up so fast, White?" he asked.

White looked at him squarely. "There were only a couple of Krauts that got around the flank and into the school building," he said. "We found them and

110

then it was easy. We just straightened out the skirmish line, and the Krauts never did make a decent attack." He grinned and held up his crossed fingers. "At least not until now."

"Well, I'm glad you're riding your squads now, anyhow," Paul said, and he was immediately sorry. After all, who was he to convey his blessings in such a pontifical way on somebody who was doing something that he himself had failed to do?

A look of resentment crossed White's face like a flash, and Paul knew he was thinking, "You son-of-a-bitch, who are you to congratulate me?" Then the look was gone and White said, "That was a nice job you did on the tank." It was an act of kindness for him to say that. Paul appreciated it and he wondered how the once feeble platoon commander had found such sudden strength.

Then he thought of more practical matters. He told White, "I'm pulling in your flanking platoons a little so you can shorten up your front. I know you've had pretty heavy losses in this squad."

White said, "I'm planning to push ahead in a few minutes. I'm sorry we got so snarled up this morning." He stood straight, almost as if at attention; chin up, looking straight ahead of him.

Paul said, "If you need anything let me know. I'm going to shove on." As he left, he was thinking, "My God, what a difference in the man! He doesn't seem like the same person. Something must have come over him during the day." And the inner voice said, "Just as something began to come over you today."

He thought about that as he started for the third platoon on his left flank. Apparently the third platoon hadn't been encountering too much trouble, for the noise had been fairly restrained from that area: nothing except American arms and a few squirts of burp-gun fire. Paul was watching the windows and following the sound-power lines which led from company headquarters down toward platoon headquarters.

He had only fragmentary reports of the progress of the third platoon, saying that they were going fast enough; no complaints, no counter-attacks. And now Paul was hoping this would be a routine day in this sector; another day of pushing the squads out, business as usual with the little bunches of men who must push their way along block by block, house by house and street by street; men being killed or wounded, always; the constant possibility of being shot at; but at least no more tanks, no more counter-attack, no more surprises. Maybe it would be a routine day, in that sense, from here on.

My God! It was bad enough about Bull, bad enough to have all that trouble with the first squad; the counter-attack and the damned German tank. But he felt somehow that Jerry would have wanted him to go ahead with the business of the day, to

112

keep pushing the platoons rather than bustling back to company headquarters.

So here he was, pushing up to the squads again, hoping some unsuspected turn wouldn't throw him into the sights of some German Schmeisser man to-day, this afternoon, after all that had happened this morning.

That reminded him that he hadn't eaten anything all day. He thought he could grab a K ration at third platoon headquarters. Funny how you didn't mind being hungry when you were scared to death. Now that there was a moment of relaxation his stomach began to squinch around and cry out for even those measly orange-colored cookies and that hunk of fat that they called K ration. Probably in a few minutes when he got up to the platoon, and maybe beyond that to the squad, he would lose his appetite again, and maybe then he would lose all the composure he had gained during the day, but at least he was fol-lowing Jerry Bull's advice; he was thinking of him-self, not somebody else, thinking of the respect he wanted to have for himself and hoping he could maintain it. He had gained it once today and lost it once. Now he was hoping, while he still wished nothing would happen in the third platoon sector, that if the test came he would be able to take it, and that the restraining quality of courage wouldn't de-sert him.

At platoon headquarters they sat down and

munched K ration biscuits and a can of cheese. Of all of the K rations the cheese unit, called the supper unit, was probably the least objectionable. The meat-and-pork loaf was an abortion; the so-called ham and eggs were like a glob of oleomargarine, and the supper unit was the least undesirable. It took a hungry man to eat the orange-colored biscuits. As for the dextrose tablets which were supposed to be a dessert, Paul would have wagered that the European continent was virtually paved with them.

The platoon headquarters was in the process of moving forward, so there was no hot coffee to go with the meager meal. The first section of the quota of blocks to be covered today had been gained without any casualties and Lieutenant Milo, in charge of the platoon, had gone up forward with the squads, as a good lieutenant should. Paul was about to go back toward company headquarters, rejoicing that all was peaceful when he heard a terrific outburst of firing from the direction of the third platoon front. "My God!" he thought. "It's happening again!" There were Schmeissers and single shots of rifles, BAR's, and the crunching sound of mortars, and the heavy banging of bazookas or tank cannons.

They sat and listened while they finished their K rations, then a runner came in, out of breath, with a message from the platoon commander: "Held up by mortar fire. Need mortar squad." The message was addressed to the platoon sergeant, but Paul got the mortar squad on its way, then waited to see whether the firing would diminish. A few minutes later another message came in from the platoon commander: "Strong resistance on Phase Line C. Need a tank." That, Paul knew, couldn't be done right away. The platoon of tanks—there were two left out of five—had been shifted over to White's sector.

The sound of the firing ahead had grown louder. Paul decided he had better go forward. As he worked down the street with the walky-talkies he heard firing very close; German Schmeissers, apparently, almost around the corner. He cut through a line of houses, across a back yard, along the top of a wall, down into the street and around the other corner. They were going through a house when he heard a sudden sound, a footfall. He swung toward the sound, pulling up his carbine. There was a room on his left through the doorway. He had seen a door, a closet door, move inside the room. He said sharply, every nerve tense, every muscle ready to spring, "Come out!" And a phrase he had learned could be quite practical in Germany, *"Kommen sie hier!"*

The door swung back and, as Paul snapped off the safety of his carbine, a little German child confronted him with a tear-stained face, arms over his head in a gesture of surrender. It had been such a tense moment that Paul laughed. He said to Fred, one of the walky-talky men, "I didn't know the Wehrmacht were taking them quite that young."

Paul didn't know much German but he told the little boy, a lad of six or eight years, in German, "Don't be afraid. We aren't going to hurt you." And then, as an afterthought, he added, "Where are your mother and father?"

The boy was so frightened he didn't understand the words. He repeated the question, and the boy finally said, wiping his tear-stained cheeks, "*Im Keller.*"

"The kid says his mother and father are in the cellar," Paul told the walky-talky men. "We better shoo them out before they get hurt."

So Paul took the little boy by the hand and they went down the stairs to the cellar of the house, rifles ready. There they found four German civilians, two women and two men, sitting on the bench of a white-washed air-raid shelter chamber. The Germans' faces were twisted with fear, and they stood up, holding their arms high in the air. The little fat man in the tweed suit additionally waved a white handkerchief from one pudgy hand, in token of surrender. The Germans were so terrified that Paul thought he had better say something to set them at ease, so he said, "We do not hurt German civilians. But you must get out of the way because we are fighting a war."

Slowly the Germans lowered their hands and the fear in their faces began to fade. Then the fat man in the tweed suit straightened his celluloid collar

116

and said, pompously, "There are certain goods in the house which I would like to take with me."

Paul said, thinking that the firing was not so far away and that he was wasting his time, "Go back to the rear. You can return later for your personal possessions. It is necessary to leave the area."

The German started to say something, but Paul, growing increasingly impatient, snapped, "Shut up, you goddamn Kraut! We're giving you a break by letting you out of here. Now get going!"

The German signaled to the others to go. Then as he passed an armchair in the corner of the room he turned slightly toward it and Paul saw a Walther pistol sitting on the cushion. The German and Paul focused on it at the same moment. The German turned toward the chair, bowing as if to allow the women passage from the room. He did not know it, but Paul was watching him carefully. The women left the room with the little boy, and the German bowed again to Paul, as if to give him precedence. Paul took him deliberately by one arm and pulled him toward the center of the room. The German protested violently that he was being pushed around. Then Paul picked up the pistol and threw it in the corner of the room. He searched the German's pockets and then said to him, "You'll go back to the rear where there is a camp for civilians." He said, "By rights I should give you the worst beating you have ever had in your life, but I won't."

117

He saw the little group safely on the road toward the rear, and then started again for platoon headquarters where the sounds of firing were continuous.

"Can you beat that son-of-a-bitch?" he said to Fred, the walky-talky man. "He was planning to pull a fast one all the time." But then, as before in the day, Paul was glad he had held on to himself. It was better that he hadn't slugged the German. That would have been the fate of an Allied civilian under similar circumstances if he had fallen into the hands of Krauts. They would have beaten him with whips and pulled out his fingernails, like the Gestapo boys in those cities of France when they caught the underground leaders. But there were much more effective and legal methods of eliminating the Krauts than by yourself becoming infected with the virus. A man could at least keep his self-respect.

Paul started down the last two blocks between platoon headquarters and Phase Line C. From here on he knew he would have to watch his step.

He came upon the squad with unexpected suddenness. The men were strung out along a wall and were lying low, crouching in the shelter of the brick structure. Even the platoon commander, Lieutenant Milo, was squatting, seeking shelter. When he saw that, Paul knew it was a dangerous situation; for Milo was a brave man. The firing had halted for a minute, but from the attitudes of the men he judged that they must be at the very crux of the action.

118

Milo waved him down and he squatted beside the platoon leader. Milo said, "There's a mortar down there and he's been raising hell. Three or four landed in the street out there. They must have good observation. I wish to hell I could get the thing spotted and get some mortars up here with us."

Paul said, "I sent back a message to get up a mortar squad. Are there many Krauts out there?"

Milo said, "There seems to be a whole potful of them in the next couple of blocks. Every time we stick our necks around the corner of this wall we get shot at. If I had more strength, I'd like to work my men up the street and secure that pistol-shaped building. It's some kind of trade hall or municipal building and I think there's a whole bunch of Krauts in there. Maybe we can get them to give up. If only I can get a mortar squad up here, or maybe a tank. They asked for my two tanks to go over to the second platoon this morning."

Paul said, "Yes, I know. They had a counter-attack over there and they needed them."

"I've got to get them back," Milo said. "There's nothing that will drive the Krauts out like tanks rolling down the street toward them, provided they don't have any bazookas, and I don't think they have right here."

"Okay," said Paul. "Can't you get any people up behind the school? Maybe if you got a couple of

119

men out there it would be better for the tanks when they came, anyhow."

Milo looked up and it was then that Paul became aware of the haunted, almost fearful look in his eyes. It was not at all like Milo to look that way, or say what he did then. "What do you think I am? Crazy? I'm not going to stick people up this street with the Krauts up at the end." And he added, "I've had two casualties today already. The squad leader of this squad got drilled two or three blocks back. I'm going to wait until I get some fire power up here to support this thing."

Paul thought there was some sort of accusation in this, but he chalked it up for the moment to nervous strain, the necessity of being on your toes all the time, as a platoon leader must be. It was a surprise to Paul to find Milo cracking, Milo who had been the bravest of all the platoon leaders.

Paul said, "But the tanks might not be able to get over here for awhile. After all, I've only got two left for the whole damned company."

Milo's eyes were still frightened and nervous. "Well," he said hastily, "I can't see any way out except to wait until the tanks get over here." As he spoke, a burst of Schmeisser fire crackled down the street. It was joined by two or three Schmeissers firing from other angles, and the men crouched, following the example of their officer. Then there was a great crash near by, an earth-shaking explosion and

120

a shower of fragments of brick and masonry falling into the little alley beside the brick wall. It was a mortar.

Another explosion followed almost directly afterward, as close as the other and in the same vicinity, but on the other side of the street. The German mortar crew were feeling their way through the block, trying to find the squad of Americans. Eventually, unless something were done, the searching fingers of the mortar shells would find their target. Sometimes it was an advantage to move in a battle, even when you had to move forward. It wouldn't avail the squad anything to remain bunched up like this, crouching along the wall, waiting for the Germans to close in on them.

Then the small-arms firing let up and, in the silence, Paul heard the ping of two mortar tubes being discharged, then after the second of dead silence the crrumpp-crrumpp! of the projectiles as they landed, and the doughfoots hugged the ground. Clearly he was not going to move. He was suffering from war fright.

There was nothing to do with men like that except to lead them. Paul was thinking as he edged toward the corner of the wall, "If I can get around this corner and up behind the next house we'll be twenty yards closer to the hall where those Krauts are hiding. We've got to get the squad out of here, and we've got to get those Heinies out of the building."

He said as much to Lieutenant Milo. "Listen, Milo, we'll have to take them out of here before they get hurt. Maybe we can make that hall, and if we can get behind it those Heinies will surrender. You know how they are when you have them flanked."

Milo still looked scared, and Paul went on, "If they'll follow me I think I can take them up." He said to the men, "We've got to get out of here; it isn't healthy. If we can get up three blocks behind that hall we can probably get out all those Heinies, and at least we can get away from this goddamn mortar."

Paul didn't know, but somehow he had the feeling that this was a transcendent moment; one of those permanent things of the spirit which rises from the impermanence and brutality of the battlefield. He thought again that the physical being was transitory; but that moments of courage like this did not pass away any more than the personality of the human being perished when the body was extinguished. It was a long thought for a moment like this, but it seemed right to him that he should think of it while inching along the wall ahead of his men, wondering what would be around the corner, wondering if he could or would make it. In that short space of time he thought of Suzy and Dolores. He was thinking of his family, and of himself too; and he was discovering that the two thoughts can be the same. Really he was still carrying out the advice of his friend, Jerry Bull, to think of himself, rather than someone else, but at the same time he was thinking of the way he would look when he examined himself in the mirror, and the way his kids would feel if they knew he was coming through with the goods when a moment of courage was needed.

So he came to the end of the wall, and it was time to move. As he halted before the plunge, a flood of bullets passed down the street, ricocheting from the corner, bouncing off the walls, and he heard a few squirts of Schmeisser fire, but they seemed to come from a long distance. The sounds were almost rest-ful. They didn't seem to be in the same world with him. There was a pleasant sensation of warmth, the warmth that comes with courage, and it was stronger than the fear which had plagued him.

He waited until the burst was over, while his mili-tary mind, trained through experience—hundreds and thousands of hours of experience and training and conditioning—timed the moment when he would start that dash of twenty yards to the next house; the first step toward the hall where the Germans were hiding. When the next mortar shell came it didn't jar him as the sound usually did. He heard the ping and the crash of the shell in the street. His military instinct told him this was the moment to make the dash across the open space; just a simple swift dash across a simple open space in a simple German town, just like any other German town, and yet it exemplified the whole of the struggle of the millions of men on the Western Front.

So Paul Kreider stepped out from the lee of the wall and a bullet caught him squarely in the head.

It was the third day since Suzy Kreider had received her telegram from the War Department. She had read and re-read it countless times, and she still couldn't believe the words:

"We regret to inform you that Captain Paul Kreider was killed in action in Germany on the Third Army front. . . ."

Dolores was crying in the bedroom. It was time to feed her. As she went to the baby, Suzy was repeating to herself, "I can't believe it. I can't believe he could have died."

And it was a sort of comfort to her that she would probably never believe it. If she lived to be a hundred she would probably never believe it. And she knew that she was right: because Paul Kreider was a brave man; and she knew, as Paul Kreider had known in the German city of Unterbach, that bravery, and honor and decency, cannot and will not die.

124

Printed in the United States
26284LVS00001B/103